fresh
cuttings

fresh cuttings

A CELEBRATION OF FICTION & POETRY
FROM UQP's BLACK WRITING SERIES

Selected by Sue Abbey
& Sandra Phillips

UQP

First published 2003 by University of Queensland Press
Box 6042, St Lucia, Queensland 4067 Australia

www.uqp.uq.edu.au

Typeset by University of Queensland Press
Printed in Australia by McPherson's Printing Group

Distributed in the USA and Canada by
International Specialized Book Services, Inc.,
5824 N.E. Hassalo Street, Portland, Oregon 97213–3640

This project has been assisted by
the Commonwealth Government through
the Australia Council, its arts funding
and advisory body.

Sponsored by the Queensland Office
of Arts and Cultural Development.

Cataloguing in Publication Data
National Library of Australia

Fresh cuttings: a celebration of fiction and poetry from
  UQP's Black Australian writing series.

  1. Australian literature — Aboriginal authors. 2. Australian literature —
  20th century. 3. Australian literature — 21st century. I. Phillips, Sandra
  (Sandra Ruth). II. Abbey, Sue.

A820.8089915

ISBN 0 7022 3338 2

Front cover art by artist Minnie Pwerle (Anmatyerre),
'Awelye Atnwengerrp' (Women's Body Design) 2002.
Artist born 1910 in the Utopia region of Atnwengerrp.
Her languages are Anmatyerre and Alyawarr.

Contents

contents

Editors' Introduction

Fresh Cuttings brings to its readers a vibrant and compelling assembly of stories and indelible voices that in turns seduces and challenges. These individual 'cuttings', or extracts, have been gathered from novels and poetry collections published in UQP's Black Writing series since 1990. The series itself has evolved out of the dynamic writing community that has both been tapped and inspired by the David Unaipon Award. This annual award, named after Australia's first Aboriginal writer to be published, David Unaipon, was launched in 1988. Each year the Award judges, three established Indigenous authors, select a winner who is assured publication by UQP. Like the Award, the Black Writing series includes a wide range of writing genres, from fiction and poetry to scholarly criticism and lifestories.

In these selections there are words that might smart and words that warmly envelope. Each author writes from his or her own place in ways that connect them to others. As a compilation, the fiction and poems are drawn together by the mesmeric power of Indigenous story and its ability to acknowledge past injustices and to heal. Yet each writer walks their own path in telling their story or that story that brings their readers in, along and through. Each piece resonates with the tutelage of life.

There is the story of institutional life by Doris Pilkington Garimara, whose later book *Follow the Rabbit Proof Fence* was the basis for the film that lifted her fame onto the world stage. Here, with an extract from her first book *Caprice*, she chronicles the life of a ward of Western Australia's Aboriginal orphanage systems in the style of fictionalised memoir and family history. *Follow the Rabbit Proof*

Fence and her most recent book *Under the Wintamarra Tree* were written in the factual yet engrossing writing style of documentary nonfiction and have become formidable weapons in the Stolen Generation debate.

Retired Queensland drover Herb Wharton exemplifies the precept "write about what you know best". With his first book *Unbranded*, he wrote the story he'd always threatened his droving mates he would one day write. As with his subsequent books, his novel is replete with the political and philosophical views of a proud and self-reliant Murri man.

Vivienne Cleven's imaginary country towns are the backdrop against which she sets the tension of unruly Black lives in a White world. Her Unaipon-winning book *Bitin' Back* is farce-like comedy pitched at breakneck pace, which paradoxically provokes laughter rather than indignation. Within a year and before she could be categorised as a comedy writer, she released her next book, *Her Sister's Eye*, a disturbing tale of small town racial violence enacted on generations of local Murri families.

Plains of Promise has been published in several countries where it is lauded for its evocative portrait of Australia's Gulf Country. As well as her eye for detail, Alexis Wright possesses the skill of the epic writer ever mindful of a wider world.

Larissa Behrendt is the most recent winner of the Unaipon. As a Land Rights lawyer she is conscious of the power of language to conquer and oppress but, more importantly, to heal. In *Home*, her autobiographical story of discovering her Aboriginal family is turned on its edge to become a multi-voiced novel of going home. Like Pilkington Garimara, she adds another strong voice to the seldom revealed accounts of the Stolen Generation and the legacy of removal.

Melissa Lucashenko's debut novel *Steam Pigs*, a Highly Commended in the Unaipon Award was published in l997, and one year later claimed the Kibble Women's Writing Award. Lucashenko captures the struggle that is being young, Black female and poor. Her writing is quirky and defiant and unashamedly political. Her characters stay with you. In *Hard Yards*, her second novel, she wrote about life on the edge with a knowing compassion for the overlooked.

The poetry in John Muk Muk Burke's fiction is powerfully evident, particularly in descriptions of the land. The world of the vulnerable young boy Chris exists in a dazzling, dreamlike frame of the writer's imagination. That he has gone on to become a prize-winning poet is no coincidence.

Poetry, a natural companion for the fiction in this selection, is in the tongue of every storyteller. Over the years, poetry has been the most heavily represented writing category entered in the Unaipon Award. However, poets have only won twice. Both of those award-winning entries (*Holocaust Island* and *Of Muse, Meandering and Midnight*) appear in this selection.

Graham Dixon is the inaugural winner of the Unaipon Award. His collection *Holocaust Island* tilts at the bastions of power - big business and government - while pride in his Nungar identity sustains him. Fellow countryman and celebrated writer Jack Davis published what was to be his last poetry collection *Black Life* in the Black Writing series. It contains his trademark elements of reading the land and honouring it as his inspirational source.

The contemporary use of language and imagery in John Graham's poetry looks out onto the world, drawing us in and reminding us of our eternal connection to the earth. With the words of 'the old ones' and the stars as reference points, he advocates world harmony.

Lisa Bellear's poetry collection, *Dreaming in Urban Areas*, traverses the global yet speaks with sincerity and compassion to the individual. With seductive rhythm and unpredictable turns, she provokes us to look injustice in the eye. She also reminds us of the 'need to maintain the capacity to love'.

Samuel Wagan Watson is the most recent poet to win the Unaipon Award with his vibrant collection *Of Muse, Meandering and Midnight*. He exhilarates in the language, bending and remixing it to fit the songlines of urban misadventure. Within a year he followed it with the road poems of *Itinerant Blues*.

Recently Highly Commended in the Unaipon Award, Elizabeth Hodgson turns her poet's gaze on the struggle as well as the dignity of Koories coping with systems of imbalance and social intolerance. Her own experience informs her poetry, offering a guiding voice to those who continue to struggle with the unshakeable burden of removal from family and home.

The ultimate quality of these pieces is in their transcendent ability to empower the writer and the reader. They extend our reading experience and significantly build on our nation's literature. As inspiration to other Indigenous writers, these authors and poets lead the way, beyond tolerance and understanding or popular and academic acceptance of their work, to the hard won goal of being valued and acknowledged as vital contributors to Australia's culture and literature.

To readers who do not know them, these 'cuttings' offer the thrill of first discovery. For those already acquainted, these works, selectively picked and purposefully arranged, offer fresh interpretations.

Sue Abbey   Sandra Phillips
Brisbane 2003   Canberra 2003

BITIN' BACK

VIVIENNE CLEVEN

bitin' back

The boy is curled up in his bed like a skinny black question mark. Ain't like he got a lot of time to be layin bout. A woman gotta keep him on his toes. That's me job; to keep the boy goin. Hard but, bein a single mother n all. Be all right if the boy had a father. Arhhh, a woman thinks a lot a shit, eh? A woman's thoughts get mighty womba sometimes!

I pinch me nose closed; the room stink like it been locked up for years. I shake Nevil awake. 'Nev. Nevil, love. Come on wake up. Ya got a interview today, down at the dole office.'

'Wha … What?' He rolls over, the sheet twisted round his sweat-soaked body. He rubs his eyes and looks up at me with sleepy confusion.

'The dole office. Interview. Ya know, today. In bout thirty minutes. Come on, no use layin there like a leech.'

'Who, what?' He struggles up on his bony elbows, givin me a sour gape of bewilderment. *The boy look myall this mornin.*

'On ya bloody feet. Don't want none a ya tomfoolery today.'
I look at the beer bottles, the bong and all them books scattered on the floor. I eyeball the titles — *Better Sex, How to Channel. Shakespeare, Oscar Wilde, Ernest Hemingway. Yep, was always a mad one for readin, our Nev.*

I turn round. He's still in bed, his arms folded behind his head as he stares up at the ceiling. 'Jesus Christ! Get outta friggin bed will ya! A woman got better things to do than piss bout here all day whit you! Come on, Nevie, love.' I soften me voice to a low crawly tone. 'Mum's got bingo. Might hit the jackpot, eh?'

'Who's Nevil?' he ask, starin down at his hairy, mole-flecked arms.

'Wha …? What's wrong whit ya? Ya sick?' I peer at his face.

'I'm not sick. And don't call me Nevil!' He nods his head and his bottom lip drops over, like he's gonna bawlbaby.

'Yeah, if you're not Nevil then call me a white woman!' I sit on the edge of his bed, laughter bubblin in the back of me throat. *Was always a joker, our Nev.*

'I'm not Nevil, whoever that is!' He busts his gut in sudden anger, his hands curled into fists.

'Talk shit,' I say, waitin for the punchline.

'How dare you talk to me like that!' His voice sounds like he really true means it as he glares sharp eye at me.

'I'll speak to ya any friggin way I wanna! Now get outta bed before I kick that black arse of yours!' I stand up, me hands on me hips, foot tappin the floorboards. *Don't push me, Sonny Boy.*

He pulls the sheet up to his face, his brown eyes peepin out from the cover. 'Call me Jean,' he whispers.

'Jean! Jean!' The laughter jump out, I double over holdin onto me gut, heehawin and gaspin for breath. 'Yeah, good one Nev, bloody funny.' I take control of meself when I suddenly realise how still and quiet he is. *Not like Nevie.*

'Call me Jean — Jean Rhys, that's my real name', he says, droppin the sheet, showin his thick black chest hair.

'What the fuck …! Are you on drugs, son? Hard shit, eh?' I peer at his face, waitin for a confession. *The boy flyin high or what?*

'Nope. Just call me Jean.'

'Jean. Right, I get the joke, ha, ha, funny,' I say, takin a closer look at him but seeing nothin outta the ordinary.

'It's not funny! I can't see any humour in my name. How would you like me to make fun of you, huh?'

I walk over to the bed. 'Somethin real wrong whit ya, Nev?' I drop me eyeballs down at him. *Too much smokin pot n pissin up all that grog is what does it. How the friggin hell did he come up with a cockadadoodle name like Jean Reece, for God's sake! A woman's name!*

5

'Just remember I'm Jean Rhys, the famous writer,' he says, flashin his chompers as he picks at his nails. As though to say: 'Are you madfucked, Ma? Can't ya see who I am?'

'A writer! A woman writer! Jesus Christ Almighty! Next you be tellin me yer white!' Me hand flies to me chest, as though to stop me thumpin heart. *Weedeatin, that's what's wrong whit him. Yarndi messin whit his scone.*

'Yep, sure am,' he answers, throwin his legs over the side of the bed.

'Nevil, stop this rot! You startin to worry poor ol mum here, son. Anythin you wanna talk bout? Girlfriends, football, yarndi?' *Sometime talkin help clean out the shit.*

'Nope. Sure appreciate if you'd call me by my right name though,' he says, one hand scratchin his arse, the other rubbin his stubbly chin.

'Okay, Nevil. Nevil Arthur Dooley, male, twenty-one years old, black fella from the bush.' I give the boy a smooth n oily smile. *Gotcha! Take that one!*

'Damn you! It's Jean, Jean Reece! J-E-A-N! RHY-S! Get it!' he yells. Spit flies across the room and lands on me face.

'Oh righto, Jean. Is it miss or missus?' I decide to go along with him, to play out this little joke. *Jean Rhys, eh. Biggest load a goona a woman doned ever heard.*

'*Miss'll* do fine, thank you, Mum.' He smiles, then drops his head n looks down at the rubbish-strewn floor.

'Well, Miss Jean Rhys, what may I ask have you got in those undies there, huh?' I throw him a spinner. *Take the bait, boy. Our Nev n his jokes. A regular commeediann.*

'That's crass. What do you think's in there?' He spins round, grabs the bath towel off the window ledge and winds it round his skinny hips.

'Well … I really don't know any more.'

'Hmmpph, stupid question, Mother. Now where are my clothes?' he asks in a pissy sorta way, runnin his tongue cross his thick-set lips as he catches a glance a hisself in the mirror.

'In the wash, Nevil — I mean Jean.' I walk over and stand behind him as he stares at hisself.

'Have you ever seen such bewdiful hair, huh?' he says, his fingers tryin to comb through the baby arse fluff on top of his scone.

'Yeah,' I whisper, by this time knowin somethin is very wrong whit me only kid.

I catch his eyes and look into them, wonderin what mischief lays there. I see nothin. His eyes hold no deep secrets. I reach out and touch his shoulder. 'Tell Mum, Nevil, tell Mum.' I will him to answer me, to tell me somethin has happened, someone has paid him to pull this stuntin on me. *Ain't like Nev to be*

*aresin bout like this. Talkin mad, sorta like he got that possessin
stuff. A manwomanmanwoman. Like the boy mixin his real self
up whit another person.*

'I need a frock. A nice one,' he says, pullin faces at hisself.

'A frock! Sweet Jesus, Nev, come on, love!' I take a wonky
step back from him, feelin like as though he's done punched
me in the gut. *The boy is deadly serious.*

'You heard me. I can't very well get about in those things
there, can I?' He points to a pile of dirty jeans.

'You have before.' I try to smooth him over, 'I can get a fresh
pair off the line if ya want.' I feel somethin grip me like death
as I try to imagine me big-muscled, tall hairy son walkin round
the town in a dress.

The shock brings vomit up to sit at the back of me throat. I
realise with a sick despair that he means to wear a dress right or
wrong. *He won't back out even for me. He's mad in the head. He's
gone crazy n gay. A woman can't take it.*

Now let me see, yeah, I member that ol girl long time past,
this sorta thing happened to her. It make a woman wonder: ya
got black fellas sayin they white. Ya got white fellas sayin they
black. I just dunno what's racin round in they heads. Cos,
when ya black, well, things get a bit tricky like. See now, if ya
got a white fella then paint him up black n let the man loose
on the world I reckon he won't last long. Yep, be fucked from

go. But when ya got a black fella sayin he's a woman — a white woman at that! Well, the ol dice just rolls n another direction. Ain't no one gonna let the man ... boy, get away whit that! This here is dangerous business.

'Well ... I spose ... you'll ... fit into a dress a mine. Tell me, what's Gracie gonna think, eh?' I shake me head at him, the idea comin to me as I speak. 'She won't like it, Gracie girl, havin a boyfriend walkin bout in women's clothes. She won't put up whit it. She'll leave fer sure!' I let it all out, jabbin the air whit me finger.

'Well, too bad ain't it. Anyway, who's Gracie?' Nev turns round to face me.

'Don't talk stupid. Gracie's your girlfriend. Enough of this for once and all. I gotta go to bingo, the others'll be waitin for me. So get dressed; hurry up.'

He walks toward the bathroom, heavin his shoulders up and down as he sighs and mumbles to himself. There's somethin wrong whit the way he walks, steppin ballerina like as he goes down the hallway. Suddenly I wonder if our Nev is one a those.

One of em homos. Well, they don't call em that any more. Gay, that's the word people use. Jesus Christ! Can ya wake up gay? Must do, Nevil did. But then again some people can con theyselves that they anythin. Thinkin of that ol girl, what was her name? It were Phyllis, Phyllis Swan. If a woman's recollection is right, she were

*parted from her own mob by em government wankers; they reckon
she too white for the others, eh. Too white, load a goon. When she
growed up a bit more her skin turned up real charcoal like. Yeah,
she coloured into a piece a coal. Black as Harry's arse. The wankers
say: she too black for us, send the girl back. So back she go to her
mob. They didn't want her. The whites didn't want her. She was
sorta stuck in the middle like. Piggy in de middle.*

Now what she doned?

*Oh yeah, she done tell everyone that she's not Phyllis Swan at all!
Oowhhh noooo! She says she really the Queen a England! Conned
herself good n proper. The mad thing was, white fellas treated the
woman whit respect! Like she truly were the Queen! I swear to God
every time I seed that woman she were gettin whiter every day!
White as friggin frost. Like she believed it so much that her skin
was believin it too! Funny sorta turnout n all. Maybe this somethin like Nevil goin through. Conned hisself good n proper like.
Hope he don't start thinkin that he be the friggin Queen! Jeees-
suuss.*

Now, how I'll tell me brother Booty? He won't like it! He'll
kick Nev's arse for sure. Oh geez, what's a woman to do? It's all
Davo's fault. Yep, pissin off on the boy just like that. No father
to play football whit, play cricket whit, nothin. Spose a
woman'll have to try n get Booty to have a yarn to him. Me boy
won't listen to me. Now where the friggin hell did he get a

name like Jean Rhys? A white woman writer, geez, couldn't he a picked a black woman writer? Someone spectable like Oodgeroo? Bloody white woman me fat arse!

That's our Nev's problem, got his head stuck in all em books. Brainwashed. Them books have brainwashed him. Yeah, reckon that's bout the strength of it. Ain't no kid ever woked up whit headcrackin shit like this.

I let me thoughts go while I radar Nev's bedroom, lookin for any sign — any *gay* sign. In the corner books sit stacked up on each other, some tattered and dog-eared, others brand-new. *Well, spose he does spend his money on other things part from piss n dope.*

I kneel down and look closer at the cover pictures and titles. *Yeah, some freaky stuff here all right.* I look for anythin that might have the name Jean R-h-y-s. Unstackin the books, I run me eyes over each one. There must be somethin here. Some clue.

Then I do notice somethin, five books by the same writer. *An Ideal Husband, Salome, The Importance of Being Earnest, Lady Windermere's Fan, A Woman of No Importance.* I take in the writer's name: Oscar Wilde. A playwright, the cover says. *What the hell's a playwright?*

I flick the cover open but there seems nothin outta place, nothin that would brainwash a man into thinkin hisself a woman. Just writin. Me eyes flick back to the other book, *A Woman Of No Importance. Now that sounds a bit suss. Maybe the boy don't think he important? A Woman Of No Importance? Hhhmmm.*

Sighin, I get up to me feet decidin I've had enough of this Nevil wantin to be a woman shit. *There's only one person who can talk some sense into the boy and I'll have to go and find him. Yep, can't have Nevil walkin down the main street in a dress. Geez.*

I walk past the bathroom. Nevil's voice sings out loud and deep. 'I am woman, hear me roar!'

'Bloody wake up to yerself, Nevil!' I yell as I open the front door and step out onto the street. *Watch me roar, Jeesus Christ! What's he now, a lion?*

'He woke up like that.' I look at Booty from across the kitchen table.

'Mave, men don't wake up bein poofters. Look at me, you don't see me wantin to wear women's clothes, eh?' He sips his beer.

'I'm tellin ya, Booty, he wasn't like that yesterday. He wake up like that! Sorta like … um, whatever it is, just stayed hidin in him n jumped out this morning,' I say, flappin me arms out to prove me point.

'Jumped out, my black arse. He was always like that, Mave,

you jus never saw it is all. Women's clothes, Jesus!' Booty shakes his head, disgust washin over his fat face.

'Yeah, what bout Gracie, eh? Tell me that?'

'A cover. He's just using her as a cover. Ya hear bout all these movie stars n such, tellin the world they're queer. "Comin outta the closet", they call it. Yep, I seen all that sorta shit on Ricki Lake. Women wantin to be men and men wantin to be girls. Yeah, Mave, the boy's been watchin too much a that American shit on TV. Seems to a man that kids don't know who they are. They all wussies I reckon. Black wantin to be white; white wantin to be black. That's where all these ideas come from — TV. Like he shamed a who he is or somethin.'

'Booty, he don't hardly watch TV. Nope, all he does is read them books a his. It's them books puttin ideas into his head. Brainwashin him, Booty.' I slump me shoulders wearily.

'Well, what can a man do, eh? He won't listen to his ol uncle here,' Booty gets up from his chair and walks over to the window, shrugging his broad shoulders.

'Yeah, but it's not only that. He thinks he's a writer! A white woman writer. Thinks his name is Rhys!'

'What the …? Booty croaks, swinging round on his heels, mouth agape, a stunned look on his dial.

'Jean Rhys. J-e-a-n R-h-y-s. That's his new name, so he reckons. She sposed to be a writer. Can't say I heard a the woman. Don't read books meself. Must go n ask Lizzy at the library there. She'd know bout this woman, I betcha.'

I watch Booty's face turn a faint shade of grey, the veins stickin out on his thick neck. 'What the hell's wrong with that boy! Jean Rhys, eh. He needs a good throttlin, that's what he needs. And I'm just the man to do it! Ain't no bloody nephew a mine gonna go dancin round the town callin hisself a woman!'

Booty busts his guts, pullin out a chair with such force that the can a beer topples to the floor.

'Righto, don't go givin yerself a heart condition, Brother. All I'm askin is for you to have a good talk to him. I blame it on Davo. The way he upped and pissed off on us. That's half the trouble, I betcha,' I say, feelin me heart start to gallop as the memory of Davo comes back. *Davo, friggin scourin off like that. No wonder Nev don't know hisself.*

'Bullshit! Never worried him all these years. Why would it worry him now? Nah, the boy's got a screw loose upstairs. Only thing you can do is get him to Doctor Chin. Take a good look at that head a his. I heard a people doin some sicko things — but this! Well, this really is somethin. Bad, fuckin bad business.' Booty gives me a serious, this-is-gone-too-far look.

'Maybe yer right. Can you come over n talk to him first? See, I'm thinkin he'll listen to you.'

'Righto, Mave. Gotta stop him from gettin outside in that friggin frock. Imagine his mates n the others, specially the footie team! They'd tear him to pieces for sure! You know what this town's like, Mave. They'd pick him to death.' Booty gets to his feet. 'Ready?'

'Yeah. But I'll warn ya, it's not a pretty sight. When I left him he was singin in the bathroom bout bein a woman n roarin.' I shake me head, me own words seem unreal to me own ears.

Booty strides out in front of me. Each step he takes drives into the footpath. His shoulders hunch forward as though he's ready to tackle somebody, ready to put em into the ground.

Up at the corner shop I notice Big Boy Hinch, one of Nev's mates from the Blackouts, our local footy team. I silently pray he don't ask bout Nev.

'Hey there, Missus Dooley. Where's the Nev?' He asks the dreaded question as he shoves potato chips into his big mouth.

'Nev. Well … um … he's crook. Got a flu or somethin,' I answer, watchin the way his muscley arms ripple.

'He's crook, eh. A man'll have to get him back onto that football field, best thing for him. We got the game comin up with the Rammers next week. Hope he's right for that. Best player we got, Nev.' Big Boy smiles, football pride drippin from his eyes.

'That's our Nev. Now look, you tell em other fellas not to call round my place. Nev needs a good rest. He'll be right by next week I reckon.' I give him a wide smile, wonderin what he'd do if he saw our Nev this mornin, singin n dancin round. *Hmmph, probably tear him a new arsehole.*

'Mave! Come on, woman!' Booty yells out from the end of the street.

'Comin! Righto, Big Boy, see ya, love.'

'See ya at the game, Missus Dooley.'

'Dunno bout that,' I whisper, trottin down the road.

Nevil sits on the edge of his bed, a book in one hand, a beer in the other. A joint hangin outta his slack gob. The room smells like it's full a horseshit; Mary Jane floatin out the window.

'Nev, Uncle's here to see ya.' I notice the way his legs are crossed over each other like one of em Buddah people. He ignores me. 'Nev love, lovey, Uncle Booty's waitin in the kitchen for ya.'

'What? Who?' He asks, bringin his head up to gaze at me with bloodshot eyes.

'Uncle. He's here right now.'

'Why?' He takes a drag.

'To talk. Um … he was just goin by, wanted to see ya is all,' I take a step into the room.

'Is this about Jean, eh? Cos if it is then I'm not talking to anyone,' he answers.

'Jean? Who's Jean?' I try.

'Don't start this again, *Mother*. You know very well who Jean is.' A touch of anger to his voice.

'Oh yeah, I *forgot*.' I give him a sour I've-had-enough-of-you look. 'Nevil, what is that on your face?' I peer at him.

'Nothing much.' He reaches over and stubs out the smoke.

'*Make-up*? Nevil Dooley, is that woman paint on that face a yours!' I walk right into the room.

'So? And don't call me Nevil!' He's all pissed off n riled like.

'It's make-up! Where the hell did you get that!' I slit me eyes at him. *Face paint. Clown colourin.*

'Oh, somewhere.' He takes a sip of beer.

'Nevil Dooley! What the hell's goin on here, Sonny Jim!' I turn to the doorway. Booty blocks the exit with his large frame, his hands on his hips as he glares in at Nevil.

'Hello, Uncle. I ain't doing nothing.' Nevil gives him a wide, yarndi grin.

'Son, what the fuck is that on ya face?' Booty strides into the room, gut swingin from side to side, eyes narrowed and mouth twisted. *He gonna take a hunk a flesh.*

'Lipstick, eyeshadow, eyeliner. Reckon it looks okay?' Nevil uncurls his legs, arches his eyebrows, puckers his mouth.

'Look here, son, you can't go gettin bout like that! What are ya, a fuckin woman!' Booty tightens his mouth, a small quiver shaking his frame.

'My business. I'm not hurting anyone, am I?' Nevil reaches down by the bed and picks up a small floral-print bag.

'You got this shit from TV, didn't ya? Watchin too much American sicko shit, eh? Ricki Lake, is that it?' Booty yells, his fat arms choppin the air.

'Nope. I'm Jean Rhys, in case Mother hasn't already told you.' Nevil pulls out a tube of lipstick. 'Seductive Pink' is written large and posh like on the side a it.

'Shit. Bullshit! You a poofter now, son?' Booty walks to the edge of the bed, shoulders hunched, ready to fly.

'Don't be stupid. What's wrong with people in this house? It's as though a girl's committed some heinous offence, like murdered someone or something.' Nevil puckers up his mouth an smears lipstick cross his tyre-tread lips.

'That's it! That's it!' Booty explodes; sweat poppin out on his forehead, his veins stickin up like they ready to jump outta the man's arms as he grabs Nevil by the singlet. 'Fucken ratbag! What's got into ya? Causin ya mother all this grief! Now get into that bathroom an take that shit off ya face!' Booty shakes a crunched fist in Nevil's face.

'Leave me alone, leave me alone,' Nevil bawlbaby.

'Now you cut this crap out, son. And lay off the fuckin drugs too. Your head's fucked enough already,' Booty pulls Nevil up to his wonky feet.

'Listen to your uncle, Nev, he knows best,' I say softly.

'Yeah, yeah. Let go of me, Uncle,' whisperin weak, Nevil looks up into Booty's angry sweat slicked dial.

'Fucken no more a this shit, Nevil! Ya gotta pull that head a yours in, right?'

'Hmm, yeah, spose,' But Nevil's voice don't sound like he means it. 'Anyway, I gotta go to the dole office. So you can leave now, I gotta get dressed.'

'Now, sonny, if ya wanna have a man talk or somethin, come over ta me.' Booty pauses for a minute then says, 'But if ya gonna be keepin on at this shit, then a man's gonna have to settle ya down, n pretty fucken soon.' He wrinkles his brow, his bottom lip twitchin.

'Yeah, yeah, okay Uncle.'

'Right then, that's that. How bout a cup a tea, Mave?' Booty asks over his shoulder as he leaves the room.

'Righto.' I look behind me. *That'll sort him over. That was all the boy needed, a good yarnin to.*

Back in the kitchen Booty pulls out a chair. 'Reckon he's right now or what?'

'Dunno, spose so,' I reply, feeling sick in me gut, but hopeful.

'Geez, you weren't wrong bout him. Where the hell did he come up whit this shit?' Booty drops his eyebrows as he looks my way, his fingers tap tappin on the table.

'I dunno ya tell me. Those books gotta lot to do whit it, I reckon,' I answer, pouring the tea.

'Ain't like he had any sort of buse. You know, bashin kids so they wind up bein pissed up in they heads. Nah, ain't like he was brought up like that, eh Mave?' Booty nods and takes a sip a tea.

'No, Boot. Never had a hard life like us fellas. Wouldn't know what it's like to be so hungry you'd eat a dead horse. Nah, whatever it was it comed on him just like that. Sorta like some nightmare he can't get out of.' I sigh and then this thought comes to me sudden like. 'Boot, do ya reckon Nev was meant to be born a girl? Like … um … he's got too much woman in him stead a man? Like he's a bit man n mostly woman?'

'A sheila! Jesus, Mave! The boy's got nuts, for cryin out loud! The only half woman he's got is up there in that mad head a his!' Booty's stomach shakes the table as he splutters and gasps, laughin loudly.

'Orh. Well … ' I stop as I hear a small sound in the hallway. I turn round in my chair. 'Jesus Christ!' I stifle a scream in me throat as I gawk at the sight before me. Nevil slides long the hall, frocked in me bright red dress, his face covered in make-up, on his feet a pair of dirty, fallin-apart sandshoes. He grins idiot-like as he stares back at me, holdin tight a handbag to his chest

'Hey, Mum,' he mouths, creepin, his back gainst the wall.

Booty jumps up to his feet. 'Done fuckin told ya!' he roars. As fast as his big body can move he rushes forward and tackles Nevil, gut-section, bringin him to his knees.

'Mum, Mum, get him off!' Nevil squeals, hittin Booty on the back whit his handbag.

'Help me, Mave! Get him to his room!' Booty shouts, holdin Nevil's arms to his sides.

I stand up on shaky legs, uncertain as what to do. Then Booty pulls Nevil up by the dress and shoves him down the hallway.

'Let go! Let me go! Jesus, Uncle, let me go!' Nevil's voice cracks like a teenage girl as he struggles.

'Can't do that, Sonny Jim!' Booty growls.

I run up behind them and watch as Booty throws Nevil into his room and slams the door.

'Have you got a key?' he gasps.

'Yeah, I have. What ya gonna do, Booty?' A sick sussin grips me.

'Lock him in. Can't have him goin down the street like that, can we? Jeez, Mave, what'll the town think?'

I hesitate for a moment, 'Um … yeah, all right,' I answer, handing over the door key, but not liking the idea at all.

After Booty locks the door Nevil starts screaming from the room, so loud that I can only hope me neighbour Missus Warby don't call the boys in blue.

'Let him sweat it out. Don't worry, Sis, he'll come out of it. We just have to wait is all.' Booty puts a hand on me shoulder.

'It's not right, Booty, is it? Lockin a grown man in his room,' I feel guilty, sick at heart.

'No, it's not, Mave. But it's for his own good. They'd kick the shit outta him out there on the street.'

'Yeah, yeah, I know. But I think Nev can handle hisself pretty good when he wanna.' *I can only hope.*

'That's not the point, Sis, they'd mob him, ya know that.' Booty looks tired out, slumpin his shoulders forward. 'Mave, I can't fight the bloody town for him.'

'Yeah, Brother, true. Well, I'll see what he's like this arvie, eh?'

'No, leave him in there. Maybe he'll wake up tamarra n be back to hisself. Wait and see what happens,' Booty throws over his shoulder as he goes out the front door.

Going into the kitchen I hear Nev singin, this time bout

being a lost soul or somethin. I sit at the table, drop me head into me hands and think back, tryin to find some clue as to where this all began.

ITINERANT BLUES

SAMUEL WAGAN WATSON

the thousand-yard stare

for Loretta

I remember Lou-Lou in a blue sarong
and a tow-truck driver
                              whose dirty jokes couldn't go wrong,
'cause at the beginning of the journey
                                        there are no bad memories
                                                of roadside love

but now, I've got the thousand-yard stare
'cause the breakdowns are just too frequent
                              stuck out here
                                        on a fractured highway of angst

there's no more emergency phone calls,
the dial-tone has gone cold,
                                        dead as the bitumen
no longer can I pick from the tar
                                        inklings of love

so now, I've got the thousand-yard stare
                                    down the endless road in my
head
that I have to walk back alone
                        retinas burning
                            flanked by a red, rabbit-jacked landscape
while the crows swoop and pick
                        I'm wanting to say sorry, for all those breakdowns
I was just going blind
                        and now, on my own
                                            it's hard,
finding it hard
                        finding my way home

gasoline

you just know where it will lead to —
the prelude of a lingering kiss
upon the fumes of a heated and ravenous breath

and you're already a weary veteran of this road

'cause it's going to combust,
the spirits of her mouth
entering yours
with that *NO NAKED FLAMES* tattoo
falling from her lips
into the curves of her chest

the fragrance of a weathered fuel tank

                                        leaking unleaded desire

three-legged dogs

I live in a neighbourhood
of physically-challenged canines

tough, three-legged dogs roam the streets,
taking every day as it comes

staunch tripods of muscle and mut
still as big, still as mean, just less maneuverable

the gutters, pot holes and cars give no concessions
and a local council doesn't even provide special amenities

three-legged dogs caught in a vicious trilateral world
of the right, the wrong and the cheated

hoping to greet in doggy dreaming

                                    a warm, little pile of legs

scenes from a getaway car

another late Thursday night … and I'm wondering,
why I bothered to use expensive cologne
when the stench of the bar drowns it out

me and four other passengers tonight …
in the getaway car …
escaping the crimes that eat us away,
one of my brethren looks at my dark-skinned gait
I acknowledge his staunch Mediterranean jaw,
lines in his face like a topographic map
the cuneiform of worry, from the old country and centuries of
killing

here she comes! fake blonde along the linoleum counter … this
    driver that calls everyone 'love'
how are ya, love?
what will it be, love?
'nother pot, love?

she's at the wheel now … this getaway car of many campaigns …
    used, abused, restored and rigged
and everyone wanting a window seat

you can name your poison
but you can't choose who'll sit next to you

and Christ! the punter on the other side
he's got a face like the dartboard in a country pub
he's taken a few hits over the years
he'll definitely be in for a long run tonight
an interesting companion for this trip

then the driver asks me what cologne I'm wearing
what ya been up to, love?
what ya been doing?
and suddenly I'm riding shotgun in the passenger seat
getting death stares from four lonely men,
all dreaming of 'love' and that supermarket blonde rinse

everyone taking in the fumes of the bar
as they do every other night between the blue flashes
of either greyhounds or trotters
and the fading smell of lamb chops and countermeal mash

everyone running and trying to win
on two legs and all-fours
bets on
       bets off

the finder's fee

it's a dark little shoebox
of some human conditions,
the negative housing of thoughts, memory and pictures
of that single moment
that changed you
forever,
      that finding of a body
the refuse of an evil act
                          milky dead eyes upon your living
and what you inherited
in that pool of blood and membrane
never fading but swirling
within midnight's plague

the unconscious rituals and lusting
                      to hold that person
                             you were before,
before someone renovated the inside of your head
so more dead bodies can be stored there,
or just replications of that same body maybe

one on top of the other

a light bulb left gently swinging in the center of the room
hanging
playing that same early morning glow
over and over
the picture of a thousand dark words and sins

a scene that money can't buy,
                     a finder's fee that can't be claimed

STEAM PIGS

MELISSA LUCASHENKO

steam pigs

Two days later the night air is still and muggy again as Sue hesitates at the bottom of Kerry's wooden steps. They're newly painted the colour of Arnott's Arrowroot biscuits, and there's small pools of the pale yellow looming out of night, visible on the concrete slab at the bottom where the paint has dribbled. Foetid January presses in around Sue, making her headache worse as she prepares the story, and she's thinking storm clouds, big storm clouds meaning rain and changes, cool breezes and long-awaited relief, purple storm clouds on my face, billowing everywhere but where's my storm sistagirl, as she trudges up to the front door wishing for a drink of cold water and a different life. Here goes fucken nothing. Or maybe everything. Footsteps are heading for the door even as Sue bangs on it.

"Hi dere stranger, come on in, we got the door shut so the dogs won't come in and sit on our posters. Hot enough for ya?"

Janet greets Sue. The half-dozen women in the room are less than diplomatic, and Sue can't help noticing the sharp intakes of breath from Angela and Ky. She stands still for a moment fronting them all under the fluro light that's attracting brown moths.

"What happened to *you*?!" someone said from the corner of the room. Sue's tone is light but not too light about it. "Oh, there's this fucking idiot at training called Alex, can't pull his punches. It's the second time it's happened. I should punch his head in next time."

"Honest?" asks a woman called Anne, from where she's paused above a wet poster.

"Yeah, course."

"Well why do you go if you get hit a lot?"

Sue looked at her, struggling for the right answer.

"Oh, it's only about once a year. Gives ya the shits when it happens, but I tell ya, had a headache all day yesterday, and ya know how hot it's been."

Anne and the others nod sympathetically and begin a debate about where and if martial arts fit into feminist philosophy, as Sue gets herself a paintbrush and studiously avoids meeting Kerry's gaze. The room's full of women talking loud and telling jokes, so it's easy to remain out of the way, even with a black eye you could see from five miles off. Apart from asking her if it hurts, the others leave off Sue as a subject, which suits her right down to the ground.

Half an hour later, Kerry's finished her work and is standing in the doorway, silently watching, sucking on a fag every few seconds and sighing deeply. Jee-ssus. I knew he was just another dumb Eagleby cocksucka, but ah, shite, a person shoulda known better, eh. When Sue's just about finished and ready to hang her poster out Kerry throws her butt over the verandah and strides into the room, tanned arms gleaming with summer's six o'clock sweat. She has a look at what Sue's painted, carefully not commenting on her fading bruises that have puffed her cheekbones out in purple and brown bas-relief (she'll talk when she's ready to, otherwise she wouldn'ta showed tonight). Oh, I could be real smart if I wanted to, she thinks, like since when did a single accidental punch in the eye give you a fat lip as well, but no.

"Hey ho, smoko time!" yells Angela from the kitchen, and the others cheer her on when she brings a tray of fresh choc-chip and macadamia bikkies in. The warm baking smell fills the room, mingling with the wet paint.

"Yummo, Ange, you're a bloody genius woman." Kerry grabs biscuits in both hands and munches away. The others laugh as the crumbs scatter.

"Howdja stay so skinny, Ker? You've always got something in your face," Janet asks cheerfully. Kerry looks shocked.

"Me! I *never* eat!" and the others all crack up. "Oh, well, maybe now and again … and how about you Suse, don't you want one — they're beautiful?" Kerry shoots her a look worth at least a thousand words, if not an entire book. Sue gets flustered.

"No thanks, I'll be right, I'm getting so fat anyway …"

"Ah, fat shmat. Garn, don't worry about it, they're really, really nice." Kerry insists.

"No, no …" she trails off and Ange buys into it.

"My slaving away in the hot kitchen not good enough for you, eh? Go on, Sue, just have a taste." Sue can tell that she's drawing more attention by not eating, so she takes one and delicately bites into the edge.

"What do you think?" Ange asks, fishing for compliments.

"Mmmm, really nice." Sue forces a smile, hiding the biscuit in her hand, and getting up to go for a glass of water. Kerry follows her into the empty kitchen, gets the panadol down off the top of the fridge and hands it to her young friend, then shuts the door dividing the kitchen and lounge.

"You alright?" Kerry asks quietly but pointedly. "Gotta sore lip eh? Or is it a cracked tooth? C'mon Sue, the others might believe you but you can't bullshit me you know."

"What'dja mean bullshit …" Sue begins to protest furiously but Kerry's face stops her. In her teenage shame she tries once more to hold it precariously together, then her face crumples. Kerry rushes forward, and Sue — untouchable, hardhearted, never-to-be-hugged-or-touched Sue — clings to her like she's a life raft, shaking with sobs, the tears streaming down in silent rivers of self-reproach.

"I feel so fucken stupid, so stupid, you know, so fucken *dumb*," she keeps saying over and over, Kerry replying "you're not, you're not" — a tit-for-tat that accurately mimics Sue's seesawing emotions. When she's cried out a bit more, Kerry steps back holding her two hands.

"Look at me, now, sis. C'mon, look at me."

Sue's head comes slowly, reluctantly up and she stares bleakly into Kerry's hazel eyes.

"It's *not your fault*. Tell me that, it's not your fault." She can't, it sticks in her throat like glue. "That's the way they get ya, you know it girl! It's *not your fault*. Say it." Kerry's eyes are relentless, and all of her considerable power is shining out of them. Sue whispers the mantra, uncertain. She squeezes her eyes shut in disbelief. Ah, God, shame, just let me die right here and now. And my *head*.

Kerry hasn't moved. "Again."

"Oh, Ker, just fucken leave it, eh? I can handle it, okay."

"Sue, you know, almost any other time I'd say yeah, you can handle it, and 'smatter of fact you will, I know that. But I looked after someone in a refuge once who asked me to just let her sit with it for a little while, so I did. Her husband got her the next day with a .22, so you'll just have to excuse me if I don't let this go."

"You never told me that." Sue's head has come up in horror-interest.

"Well, I have a hard enough time forgetting it as it is, so I don't tell that story much." Kerry is breathing steadily, arm's length away from her friend, about to insist on more words when there's a knock on the door.

"Yo!" Kerry calls out.

"It's Ange, you okay in there?" Kerry looks inquiringly at Sue, who nods.

"Yeah, come in."

Angela walks in with the tray scraped clean of biscuit dough, ready to dump it in the sink. "What's going on?"

Kerry shrugs.

"Nothing much. Eh, Sue?" Sue gets a burst of inner strength from somewhere and looks at Angela.

"I didn't get hit at training, Ange, my boyfriend did this the other night."

Ange is surprisingly unsurprised. "I wondered actually ..."

looking at Kerry like she's seen it a million times before. Kerry raises her eyebrows but says nothing.

"Well, you wondered right!" Sue says almost happy now her secret's out.

"We should troop down there and give it to the bastard!" Angela remarks savagely, "Show him what it's like to be on the other end." Sue's eyes widen in horror even as she thinks in confusion, but he does know …

"Somehow, Ange," Kerry interjects slowly, "I can't see that being what Sue's asking for here. Am I right?"

Sue manages a small laugh, and agrees. "I'm buggered if I know what I *do* want, but I know that ain't it!"

Kerry grins and squeezes her shoulder hard. "We'll have a talk later. Hokay, sistagirl, let's hang these posters then? I'll put the jug on. Ange, can you ask who's for tea?" Ange and Sue disappear out into the lounge, both a little wiser than before.

"Where's Rache tonight?" Sue asks Kerry on the verandah when the working bee has finally straggled to an end, not wanting to leave, and hoping Kerry'll have some energy to spare her.

"Up at uni using the library I think, unless she went around to Kate's that is. She lets me have the house to myself when we have lots of people around." Kerry fiddles with the hanging crystal pendant that catches the sun in the mornings and turns the lounge into a rainbow. "Do you want another cuppa? I reckon it'd do you good, mmm?"

"Yeah, me too," Sue admits. So they go back inside and Sue perches on an old wooden chair watching Kerry light the stove with the clicker-thing no one can come up with a name for. Sue hunts fruitlessly for the right words.

"So. Will I start or will you?" Kerry stands facing her, a white cup in each hand on the other side of the waist-high counter.

"Oh … shit … I dunno …" Sue trails off, shame again.

"When'd he do it?"

"Mmmm. Coupla days ago. Tuesday night. You know after the Three Monkeys, I got home that afternoon and he never got home till fucken midnight, forgot it was my birthday, can ya believe it?"

Kerry looks at her in disbelief, half-making a mental note to remind Sue about the cockatiel that Rachel had inconveniently fallen in love with.

"That's horrible, forgetting your birthday!"

"Yeah, I know, that's how I felt. Then Tuesday night I lost it when I asked him where he'd been and he lied, said he was at his mate's all night, but I'd rung Lee up and I know he wasn't there … what do you believe, Ker? I mean, whaddya do?" Sue's face is a picture in misery and defeat, and Roger's words of a fight months ago still echo in her head, '*oh, if I was pissed I'd probably fuck anyone ...*' She'd shrugged it off at the time as irrelevant, but now she wasn't so sure.

"Not for me to say what to do, girl, you make your own decisions, you know that," waving away Sue's dismissive gestures, "what bothers me is that you think it's your fault. How do ya come at that one?" Kerry's face is hard and soft at the same time, somehow, and Sue in the midst of wishing herself dead is flushed with admiration for her.

"Aw, I don't really think that. Just, just ... you know he's got a lot on his mind, and he smokes a lot of dope, he just loses it sometimes I think, it's like it's not him at all, it's someone else, you know? He's a good bloke, really, when things work they really work well. I just can't figure it out, like when he's in a mood there's nothing I can do that's right, or good enough ..."

"Yeah, I know alright ... listen, Sue, I don't care if it's Roger or fucking Adolf Hitler who done that to you, it's not *your* fault, okay? No woman ever deserves to be bashed, ever. No excuses. What?" catching Sue trying to say something but not managing to get it past the gates of language.

"I was gonna say, oh, it's like it's part of being Murri, you know, you expect it ..." Sue blurted into the silence.

"Uh-huh. Right." Jesus, how to tackle that one. It was comments like this that made Kerry, whitegirl that she was, wonder what she was doing in such conversations. "Sue, when they took your granny away, what was that for? Cos she was black, right? And when your mum wouldn't ever talk about it, when she brought you up denying it, what was that for?"

"She thought it was to protect us, I guess, so we didn't have to go through what she did." Sue answered, puzzled, I know this shit. "Look, this isn't because I've got some big identity crisis, you know —" regretting the day she'd sat around with Rachel and Kerry telling them how she'd been brought up white and how much it hurt when other Murries reminded her she had a family of coconuts and just incidentally was nothing herself, by the way. Or when the powerful Torres Strait woman had asked, And where are you from? like she didn't know the old, old story and how to dig where it really pained.

"Hold on a second, and then you can convince me of that," Kerry interrupted her brusquely. "Just tell me one thing." She paused to put her cup down and stare at Sue. Looking straight at her she popped it, "If Roger was white, would you put up with this?" Sue is silent, absorbing the implications. "Cos if your identity, no, not your *identity*, if your response to what the whites tried to do in making you white, if that's gonna make you put up with being flogged, well, you tell me …" Kerry stares Sue down, not angry with her, but angry with a system that could do this to people, fucked up Murries all over the damn country. Land — *gone*, families — *gone*, dignity — *gone*, culture — *gone* — and Ker ablaze with that anger till Sue expected to see sparks flying out her head into the night sky, bursting against the stars, popping red and yellow and hey, black, that'd make it the Murri colours, but isn't that the problem in the first place, colours and divisions and flags and whose side are you on boys, and o, what the fuck …

"I dunno." Sue looks blankly at her friend, worn out with emotion. Kerry's face relaxes.

"Yeah, you do, girl. You know. And you know what else?" Sue's head rearing up again in query. "You've got friends, hey?" Sue smiles back, yeah I know, sort of, and Kerry tells her, "You and Rache, what a fucking pair of steam pigs, I dunno, I must have a magnet or something." There's a twinkle in her eyes as she starts humming an old song "*pigcity, uhuh pigcity*", and washing up the cups. It works. Sue forgets her worries in curiosity about what a "steam pig" might be.

"A pair of what? Pigs?!"

Ker laughs at Sue's bewilderment. "Don't get your knickers in a knot. I didn't say 'pig', I said 'steam pig'. Quite different. It's railwayman's talk for something that doesn't fit properly, a square peg in a round hole. A mongrel. Something not really definable, you know? A white blackfella, or Aussie Jewish dyke brought up outside her faith. Rache is one cos she goes through life knowing that *real* Jews live in New York or Manchester, and thinking what business has she got living with 1. *a goy*, 2. who's a woman, 3. in Beenleigh, 4. *Australia*, 5. not speaking her language, need I go on …? She knows she's not a gentile but she sure as fuck don't feel like no Jew … and that, I'd lay good money, is pretty much the way you fit, or rather don't fit the picture, am I right or am I right? Like you've got the white skin (Sue is insulted, she's at least olive) and the good English and the grade twelve education and you read books and you grew up white and you've got the beginnings of an extremely shoddy feminist analysis — hardly classic Aboriginal stuff, is it?" Growing more vicious, Kerry prods her a bit, "But aaay, she's got a black boyfriend, ridgy didge off the mish, sista, so she must be blaaaack, hey? And he gib her a bitta blackfella loving every now and then, well that just goes to prove it, dunnit?"

Sue snaps back, irritated. "Fuck that, now you're blaming me, same as he does —"

"Uhn-uhn, no way, his fist, his fault. I'm just saying you're confusing colonisation with culture, and blackness with oppression. See the same thing in Rache all the time, my immediate family wasn't gassed so I can't be a real Jew. So now she goes overboard. It's manipulative bullshit that whites use to fuck minorities all the time, internalised oppression, letting us define what makes you who you are, and till you get over this hurdle, your whole life is going to revolve around being fucked up one way or the other. What you've more or less said is what most whites think, too, that there's nothing more to being Aboriginal than drinking and fighting and being poor ... but that's just the garbage we've given you since Cook arrived. You could live in a palace and still be a Murri in your heart. Course, you wouldn't live there by yourself, probably!"

"So when did you get to be the fucken expert on this, honky?" Sue asked, a bit more calmly, sipping her tea.

"Hey, if you live with someone twentyfourhours a day, you learn more about their shit than they know themselves. Not that I'm any expert. But it's classic stuff, Sue-me-blue. And now, sorry to say, I'm buggered, and need me beauty sleep." Kerry drains her cup and jumps to the floor. "Do you wanta stay here tonight? You can crash on the spare bed if you like. In fact, you can stay for longer if you want to look for somewhere else to live ...?"

"That'd be good, yeah, thanks." Sue, busily thinking about what Ker has said, is uncertain about moving out of her unit, but is grateful for the offer to stay the night.

Kerry settles her guest into the small room, Sue pleased at the opportunity to let Rog worry about her whereabouts for a change, the sexist bloody cocksucker, let *him* think *she's* out screwing around. And maybe Ker's right … maybe she should leave … but she still loves him, and they've only just moved into Hillside Drive, it seems so stupid to shift out now … still, he hasn't got any right to go hitting her …

The room's cosy and full of books, and when Kerry turns Sue's light off at midnight, the new *Our Bodies, Our Selves* paints a picture sprawled across Sue's stomach as she snores gently, domestic violence and the rest of it forgotten till morning. She dreams though, nasty dreams about being lost, and missing vital planes, just about missing them, that is, she usually caught what she chased in her dreams but it took a long sorry while to do it. After a while that dream fades to a nicer one about dogs and cars, and swimming out at the back of Beenleigh with people from up home. Even that one had a sinister undertone though, since her sister Deb was there shooting up on the river bank, and Sue was just shaking her head, watching her do it.

DREAMING IN URBAN AREAS
— WHITE MAN APPROVAL

LISA BELLEAR

break the cycle

Hit
me
again
and
i
swear
i'll
call
the
cops/
brother
got
to
stop
fightin'
me
i'm
your
sister

historical journals

(for Tony Birch)

Historical journals offer frameworks
to
       rationalise
       demystify
and
       historisise
constructs of deception
Reference points
are
       neutral
       safe
settler • explorer • coloniser • drovers • dyke

Reach for truth

souled out

Only $200 — Ladies/
Gents and you could
Become an Aborigine
For two whole days!
Hey lady, what's sar matter
Haven't you seen
One before?
Come and experience
The lifestyles and
Mystical spirituality
That is quintessential
To the life and existence
Of a Traditional Aborigine
We'll also have a real
Properly initiated Elder
Who will empower you
With Dreamtime secrets
From an ancient culture
And for an extra fifty bucks
We'll throw in some

Real live witchetty grubs
And eat them, just like
The Natives did all those
Dreamtimes ago.

travels on a train: 1

Hey, you don't mind if I drink?
Got a couple of spares — no!
Would you have a cigarette … and a light?
Sure you don't want a charge — eh,
Oh your missus would kill you?
Well what about me, left the Kings Tavern
In Sydney, round 5.00am, caught a train
Stopped in Penrith, then on to Katoomba
Wanted to see me little girl, and me
Mother-in-law wouldn't let me in the house,
Here, have this, cost me $48.00, na go on,
Brought up me wife's favourite VSOP.
Damn, so, I'd had a few drinks, big deal.
She just stood there, blocking the steps, between
Me, my little girl, and me ex missus. Look, for awhile
I gave up the grog, for two months and one week,
Even found steady work on a building site, that
New complex, well I come home one day and there
Was my missus, getting down with another bloke.
I followed that court order, work and don't drink

And that's what happens, used to bring me pay packet
Home unopened, true! And I ask what's left for me?
She goes running home, takes the kid, end of story.
Sure you don't want the brandy …
Thanks for the cigarette.

inevitability

A black brother dies alone
A black sister weeps aloud
There was a vision
There were dreams
And then came colonisation

A black child is removed
from her black family
and their black families white/
black/friends and 'lations

For their best/own interest
black child cries alone
black child weeps inside

A white adoptive mother/father/
brother/sister ignore the young
cries   pain   grief

Black child dies   alone
And still we
are removed …

a suitcase full of mould

Imagine alienation
Imagine a bonding process of
23 years of lies,
Of 23 years of guilt
Of being estranged
Of trying to let go ...
Of wanting to but ...

Imagine being 12
Of being home and sick
And have someone who you trust
Or someone who you think you trust ...
Imagine not being able to tell,
Of wanting to
But you have no one to tell

Hey where are all the social workers,
When you need them,
Or when you think you do.

Imagine being 13,
Coming home from boarding school
To care for a person
Called mum who has once again collapsed
Too much booze,
Too much mental torture
Too much, too much, too much

Try being 14 and look out
Your lounge room window,
It's dark now but someone who you love,
Or someone who you think you love
Is gardening
Imagine gardening at 9 pm
What is her fascination
With the gladiolies, the daffodils,
Those beautiful blue, pink and purple petunias

Oh that's right there's beer cans
Strategically placed in different
Sections of our beautiful beautifully
Manicured flower beds.

They say flowers grow for beauty
No, not for me
Flowers grow to hide
The inability to cope
Too much, too much, too much

Forget forget forget
As much as I try
I cannot, there must be
Some reason, some reason
Why so many, so many
Koories, Noongahs, Murries, Nungas,
Go through
The nightmare

Why, why, why
I don't know why
All I know is here I am at 23, 24 at
26, 36 and 46
If I live that long
I'm wondering, searching, questioning
I don't know why
Should it matter, I'm one
Of the lucky ones

A suitcase full of mould
Contains those few precious memories
Of my years, without my people
The photos
The children's books
A painting of a lighthouse I drew at 12
Short sharp memories
A collection of
My life which,
If I could have a child
If I wanted to, I would
Give to them

Hey tell us about
Your life growing up …

A suitcase full of mould
Is my childhood
A suitcase full of mould
A suitcase full of mould.

CAPRICE

DORIS PILKINGTON GARIMARA

caprice

In 1947, Kate Muldune was seven, old enough to start school, so she was transferred to the schoolgirls dormitory. The kindergarten had been her home since she was two years old. It cared for all the children aged six years and under and the conditions there were better than anywhere else on the Settlement. The food was adequate: pots of soups and stews, daily supply of milk, dried or tinned fruit and tinned vegetables. The children thrived on the loving care given by the white sister-in-charge and her dedicated staff. The children were doted on and cuddled often, no one missed out. Kate still remembers the smell of Lifebuoy Soap at bath-times.

The schoolgirls dormitory was an overcrowded, dilapidated, vermin-infested building. The beds were covered with mattresses filled with coconut hair or husks, no sheets, just government-issued rugs. At night the beds were pushed closely together, the older girls at the ends protecting their younger relatives in the middle. During the winter, spare mattresses were thrown over the blankets for extra warmth.

"The big girls told us that the dormitory was built on a cemetery or an old yard, and that every night ghosts wandered around the dormitory seeking revenge on the violators of sacred ground," said Kate.

"If we wanted to go to the toilet bucket at night, a small fire of coconut husks or fibre was lit. Still you glanced nervously around before you sat down over the bucket," she added.

The girls were locked in every evening at six o'clock and confined there until sunrise the next morning.

"The food was terrible. The watery stews were made from mutton or sausages that tasted slightly off, with unsliced cabbage leaves floating on top, potatoes and sometimes carrots," said Kate pulling an ugly face. "Weevilly porridge was sweetened with molasses or sugar if it was available. There was at least one redeeming factor, and that was there was always plenty of hot fresh bread, baked daily at the bakehouse, and of course big mugs, or in our cases fruit or Nestles milk tins, of sweet tea. The same fare was served daily and seldom varied.

"You ate the food served to you or you starved, and you said grace before you sat down to eat a meal.

"It was always the same prayer, 'For what we are about to receive may the Lord make us truly thankful. Amen.'

"What I hated most and it always makes me want to puke when I think about it, sometimes we had tinned fruit and custard. Custard indeed, it looked and tasted like lemon coloured glue. Yuk," said Kate looking positively ill.

The girls were awakened at 5:30am rain, hail or shine. After breakfast they bathed and dressed for school. Most of the children enjoyed attending classes in the two-roomed school. The infant school (pre-primary) was attached to the kindergarten. Their teacher was Miss Chapman, a slightly built lass with short curly brown hair. Miss Hillman, a very large middle-aged woman with very short curly grey hair, was also the headmistress who taught upper levels (standards 3-8), while a sturdy, spry Yorkshire woman, a Mrs Brinkley, took the lower primary levels (standards 1-3). Mrs Brinkley's class sat at long oaken desks — four to a desk — with individual inkwells.

"I had the most difficult time — I suppose the same as many of my classmates, trying to write with a pen and ink," said Kate. "I don't know how many times I got hit across the knuckles, with a command to 'hold it straight'. They gave up in disgust. 'Kate Muldune you'll never learn,' they said.

"I hated the bloody pens, I am glad we have biros now."

The availability of a formal education was seen by inmates not as a privilege but as a right, one to replace the birthright that was taken away from them. All the children looked forward to school because it was a place where pupils could forget their degrading living conditions and their horrible meals and concentrate on more important and far more interesting subjects. Apart from the three Rs there were stories to be heard, stories not about Dreamtime heroes, but about the European heroes such as William Tell, Robin Hood, the Scarlet Pimpernel and others. There were tales of the adventures of *Black Beauty*, *Robinson Crusoe* and *Treasure Island* and more. Myths and legends of foreign countries replaced the mythical beings of their traditional culture.

Now their mythical beings had names like fairies, elves, witches, goblins and hobyahs. These appeared to be more real to the children because there were colourful pictures of them in many of the books available at the school. Kate's education was constantly expanding.

The standard of education was equal to all other state or government schools in Western Australia. This was indicated by requests from the school inspector Mr Thornton for samples of work done by pupils at the Settlement school. The pupils were being groomed to become "model citizens" to be placed in positions of responsibility that would enable them to take their places in any level of society — or so they were told.

The school was the venue for all social functions, such as the monthly dances for the adults from the compound and the camps. The children watched on with delight as the old people danced around the floor. School concerts three times a year were very popular. The pupils enjoyed showing off their skills as performers as they sang, danced and acted out mini dramas. Despite the fact that these performances were solely European-oriented, the children always enjoyed the audiences.

Instruction on survival skills and bushcraft remained a recreational activity. Whilst the speaking of traditional language was forbidden, and the women would never observe or participate in religious ceremonies, rites and rituals, the myths and legends would always be in their hearts and stored away in the back of their minds, awaiting that special moment when they would be recalled and passed on to others. To ensure this, Kate's substitute and surrogate mothers who gave her maternal protection became her tutors. The forbidden topics were whispered in hushed tones in the privacy of the dormitory in the evenings or discussed on the grassy banks near the river under the shade of the huge river gum.

Everyone was acquainted with all residents at the Settlement, so it was not uncommon to see groups of women and girls heading off in all directions to forage for berries, roots and tubers — this was a regular event every Saturday morning. It was almost a ritual when for at least once a week all females assumed their ancient roles as gatherers. The only difference

now, however, was that women from the Kimberley, the Pil-
baras and the Murchison were now gathering the traditional
bush tucker of the Nyoongah people.

Every year between May and October djubak or karnoes
were dug. These were highly prized as a food source, some were
the size and shape of new potatoes. Bohn or borna, a small,
red, sometimes hot root was plentiful, as were other smaller
tubers and roots. Berries of all shapes and sizes grew in abun-
dance — and had names like emu berries (their shape and
colour were like emu eggs), gold swan, crown wooley and the
largest of all, the sand-plain berries. They were the size of an
oval-shaped grape. Nuts and seeds were gathered and shared
amongst the inmates.

During the summer months there were plenty of fish in the
river, lonkies or wheppies and buguinge mud fish, and cob-
blers, and gilgies.

The men and boys hunted for small game such as rabbits,
porcupines and parrots and galahs. The camp people who lived
some three hundred yards from the compound kept kangaroo
dogs bred specially for hunting kangaroos and emus.

Family picnics or "dinner outs" were held on Sundays.
Adults were queued up outside the kitchen servery counter to
be given cardboard boxes of food. The contents were nearly
always the same, mutton chops, bread, jam or golden syrup,

tea, sugar and tinned milk. The men "robbed" bee hives and collected the wild honey while the women and children fished, dug gilgies (small freshwater crayfish) or caught lizards and cardars (goannas).

Local bush foods were not the only things to be introduced to the people of the north by the traditional owners of this part of the country, the Nyoongahs. They also shared their myths and legends. There were warnings not to wander off in the bush alone or go too far away, for behind every Christmas or Moodgah tree a berrijal or a charnock may be lurking. Malevolent spirits such as mummaries or wood archies prey on disobedient children who have not heeded warnings of the grown-ups and are caught wandering home at dusk or night fall.

"When we came to a Moodgah tree at dusk we'd join hands and run fast as we could. Don't you worry, fear would boost your speed up one hundred percent," said Kate.

"When we went on these Sunday 'dinner outs', it was better to take as many children as you could — you got more food. We enjoyed the weekends very much and looked forward to them. No child was an orphan then.

"But one thing I shall fear and remember always is the mournful cry of the curlew or weelow. We were told that the bird was imitating the cry of a tormented, demented woman searching for her lost children," said Kate shivering slightly. "I never forgot that legend."

Two years later the government decided that Kate and the other children would enter a new phase in their lives. It was time to abolish the protection policy and legislate a new policy — the assimilation policy. Basically the assimilation policy meant that Aborigines were expected to achieve and attain the same standards of living as their white counterparts, and they would eventually become absorbed into the mainstream Australian society and be treated equally as Australian citizens. The Settlements were closing down, becoming obsolete, and Christian missions were being established throughout the state under various denominations.

We didn't travel down directly to the Roelands Native Mission Farm but made a couple of detours because the mission authorities were unsure whether they could take the full quota. They needed a fortnight to plan and reorganise themselves. So for two exciting weeks we holidayed in Perth at what was then the Displaced Persons Camp (for refugees from Europe) at Swanbourne. It seemed an appropriate place for a vacation — to us at least — the displaced and misplaced children from the Settlements.

The Displaced Persons from Europe, or DPs our guardians

called them, and the misplaced children of Aborigines had little or no contact with each other. We were aware that these "New Australians" lived on the other side of the camp. All the girls were cautioned and instructed on what action to take if confronted by one: "Don't talk to them. Run straight to the huts immediately." Basically our fears and those of the staff had no foundation whatsoever. They were based purely on assumptions that these foreigners were all bad people, the worst kind of human beings on earth.

I can remember the first time I encountered one of them. It was one morning towards the end of our vacation. I was standing on the edge of the road watching intently for the girls to return from the canteen down the road. They were bringing some P.K. and spearmint chewing gum and lollies. The girls from Moore River took to the chewing gum instantly, it was much more pleasant and enjoyable than the "bush chewies" we got from the gum or resin found on young banksias. We chewed these long after the flavour had gone.

I heard or at least I thought I heard a man's voice; it sounded very close. I turned quickly to face the speaker and there he was. A D.P. An Eye talian (Italian) standing there grinning widely, displaying his discoloured tobacco-stained teeth. I forgot the chewing gum and ran like a frightened rabbit, and didn't stop until I was safely inside the hut.

Apart from such surprises those weeks in Perth were filled pleasantly sight-seeing, picnicking on the Swan River, Kings Park, visiting the South Perth zoo and going to the local picture theatres.

But swimming in the ocean was what we enjoyed the most — especially when we were being dumped by the big waves. We laughed at and with each other when we coughed, spluttered and blew our noses and went back for more. This was the first time we had seen the sea and found it most fascinating and enjoyable.

On the last day of our holidays we said our tearful goodbyes to our Roman Catholic friends who departed on a big bus to their final destination, the Wandering Mission near Narrogin. We wondered if we would ever meet again.

A further delay — the mission needed two more weeks, so we passed the time at the Carrolup Settlement waiting patiently for them to decide how many girls they were prepared to take in their charge. They said they would accept all of us Church of England girls.

The first thing I noticed when we arrived at the entrance to the mission was the very large sign that said "The Roelands Native Mission Farm", and written underneath was a text from the bible saying "Suffer the little children to come unto me and forbid them not for theirs is the Kingdom of God."

However, before we could be welcomed and accepted into the Kingdom of God we had to go through a cleansing process. First there was the bodily cleansing. Our long hair was shorn from above the ears, almost shorter than the boys at the mission. Nine years old, I bawled my eyes out as I watched my beautiful long tresses fall on to the floor in an untidy heap amongst the others. Then came the delousing process where our heads were saturated with kerosene. I hated that, the smell was enough to knock you out. The head lice had no chance of survival in those fumes.

This was followed by a hot bath with disinfectant in it — Dettol I think.

With the bodily cleansing completed, we were taken to our dormitories and introduced to our fellow inmates.

There were twenty girls whose ages ranged from five to fourteen, some from Carrolup Settlement (later known as the Marribank Mission) near Katanning, south of Perth, and the rest of us from Moore River Native Settlement.

We were labelled the "new girls", which only served to alienate us and cause rivalry between us and the "old girls", and we felt discriminated against because we were not "born again" Christians.

The environment at Roelands Native Mission Farm was totally different from Settlement conditions. The buildings were always clean and sparkling — almost sterile in fact — with the highly polished floors, the snow-white sheets, table cloths, and curtains in the dining room, with the fruits of the spirit sewn in green cotton on the frills. There was Faith, Hope, Love, Peace and Joy. Everywhere and everything about the place gave it an air of godliness, and righteousness prevailed.

The missionaries' aim was to save souls — and the business of saving our souls began in earnest. Our guidance along the paths of righteousness began with religious instruction that immediately took precedence over normal education. Our education in a fundamentalist religious indoctrination introduced us to the Christian virtues, principles and behaviour.

These missionaries believed in the literal translation of the bible, baptism and the power of prayer and the Holy Spirit. Their religion had no room for Aboriginal religion, Aboriginal customs and Aboriginal culture. Stronger criticisms reinforced the superstition and fear of our traditional culture. The colonial terms such as "uncivilised" and "primitive" were replaced with Christian terminologies. "Evil", "devil worshippers" and the "powers of darkness" were used when referring to Aboriginal culture.

This kind of indoctrination served only to widen the already established gulf between the traditionally-oriented and the ruralised Aborigines.

Within two or three years the missionaries had achieved their aim, many of us were converted and became born again Christians. We could memorise portions of the bible and learnt to identify quotes, texts and characters of the bible.

I believe it was through the continuous indoctrination of the Christian morality and tenets — and the constant warnings of the "wages of sin" and "wrath of God" — that all of us tried diligently and faithfully to stay on the path of righteousness and never stray off it.

With this new belief came even more heroes — though this time they were biblical. These heroes were different from the previous ones, they were real, and seemed to be either punished severely for wrong-doings or highly praised and rewarded for their achievements — always about the good and the evil.

As our Christian education progressed, our formal education fell behind the rest of the state school system. With no formal education there were no formal examinations. Whilst we made satisfactory progress and advancement in the Christian faith, we gained no further knowledge of the world in the class at the little schoolhouse on the hill.

The teacher who taught the upper primary level was un-qualified. A former Yorkshire grocer, Mr Bennett should have been called "Mr Long", because all he seemed to know about maths was long division, long multiplication and long addi-tion. His talent as an organist and musician far exceeded his skills as a teacher of the three Rs.

His wife instructed the girls in needlework and embroidery. We learnt and sang a lot of hymns, English ballads or some folk songs from the British Isles.

In the mid 1950s the education of the children was taken over by the government — the department of education. Thus once again those of us who had a fondness for different or special subjects and the desire to excel in something — even though it may have been only to please the teacher — sat eagerly and ready to absorb whatever knowledge was being imparted.

Our newness became tarnished somewhat as we settled and became accepted and recognised as "the mission kids".

HOLOCAUST ISLAND

GRAEME DIXON

when

(in retrospect)

When the colour of a person's skin
Is as unimportant
As the colour of his eyes
When politicians stop
Deceiving our people
With the telling
Of their white lies
When the breed
Sired by convicts
Cease to worship
The invader
Captain Cook
When they return
To our People
The Sacred lands
They took
When compensation
Is paid in full
For the atrocities

Of 200 years past
Then and only then
Oppressors
Will our Ancestors
Rest in peace at last.

six feet of land rights

If we never succeed in reclaiming our country
doomed to live life paying rent to the gentry
It would be a good thing if after our death day
for that six feet of earth we didn't have to pay
It would ease the pressure, on those of our kind
Poor, mourning, sad people, left living behind
It would make the last day easier to face
if that financial burden was lifted
from our poverty-ridden race
Then when the reaper comes
to switch off our lights
our souls may rest in peace, knowing
at last! Six feet of land rights.

prison

Prison
what a bitch
Brutality
Savageness
Depression
Is all caused by it
Must'a been
A wajella
Who invented this Hell
Wouldn't know
For sure
But by the torture
I can tell you

To deny
A man freedom
Is the utmost
Form of
Torment
Just for

wajella — white person

The crime
Of finding money
To pay
The Land lord's rent
Justice for all
That is
Unless you're poor

Endless days
Eternal nights
Thinking
Worrying
In a concrete box
The disease
It causes
In the head —
I'd rather
Have the pox

Because man
Is just
An animal
Who needs to see
The stars

Free as birds
In the sky
Not through
These iron bars

There must be
Another way
To punish
Penalise
Those of us
Who stray
And break
The rules
That protect
The taxpayers
From us
The reef
Of Humanity's
Wrecks.

PLAINS OF PROMISE

ALEXIS WRIGHT

plains of promise

It was already hot by seven in the morning and everyone was up and about. Errol Jipp, the missionary in charge of St Dominic's, with full powers for the protection of its eight hundred or so Aboriginal inmates under state laws, stood caught in the light of the sun streaming through the girls' dormitory window. He stood directly in front of Ivy "Koopundi" Andrews, aged about seven. She had just acquired the name Andrews. Andrews, Dominic, Patrick, Chapel, Mission — all good Christian surnames given by the missionaries for civilised living. "Koopundi" and the like would be endured with slight tolerance as long as they did not expect to use such names when they left to live in the civilised world, whenever they acquired the necessary skills.

"Your mother died this morning, Ivy," Jipp announced, looking around the dormitory. "We are all very sorry." He used his high-pitched, sermonizing voice, staring down at the bowed head with its brown curls and sun-bleached ends.

Ivy did not move but gave a sidelong glance to see if the other girls were looking. She saw they were pretending not to notice. Her glance shot across to the open window. The bird could not be seen. "It's probably gone now," she told herself. She thought of her mother — that was about all she had done since being put into the dormitory a few days earlier. How her mother screamed, and she herself had felt abandoned, alone for the first time in her life. She could hear her mother crying, following and being dragged away, still crying. She did not know what had happened to her but she had not come back again to the fence that barricaded the dormitory after she was dragged away.

"Ah well, dear, we will give her a proper service in the chapel later on today." As Jipp spoke he formed the funeral arrangements in his mind. Things needed to be planned down to the last detail: that was his habit, his way of doing things. It will be necessary to find someone to dig the hole. Could he count on one of the men to bring over a plywood coffin, if there was one already made up, or should he get someone to knock one up quickly? No good keeping bodies around too long in this heat. Another thing, these people were far too superstitious. They might all try to take off in the middle of the night, as they did last time. Better secure the gates and make sure the children are locked in tonight. But maybe not. Old Ben, who died recently, was an important man. Law man, they called him. (Heaven forbid! These people never learn.) But the woman was not from around here. A loner. A real hopeless loser.

"When you hear the bell ring after class, come over to the mission house, child. Mrs Jipp will take you to the chapel." Best to make the day as normal as possible, Jipp thought as he gave the child a slight pat on the shoulder then turned and walked out.

Everyone was talking about the crazy woman from another country that had killed herself during the night. The movers and shakers of the mission had a lot to say about her.

"If you knew so much, what was her name then?" No one knew for sure. No one would have minded if she had settled down at St Dominic's, even though she did not belong here — so long as she went about her business and didn't interfere with others. What could be the harm in that? Nothing.

But someone said she had "that look" in her eye. "Down at the store that day, remember? When you went down there for bread on ration day. You said you saw it. You told me that. Told all of us. Don't muck around looking like you know nothing now. You told us yourself — that one not right."

Another sister adds to the story: "Crazy. Crazy. Crazy one."

"Then you threw your hands up in the air. Then when we asked, you said, look for yourself."

"Well, I say, anyway she looked alright. Nothing wrong. But then I must have made a mistake. Seein' she goes and kills herself."

Another voice: "Just like that. You must have known that was goin' to happen. If you could see something wrong with her. You should have done something to stop it. Poor woman might still be with us now. Instead of waitin' to die. Waitin' for spirits to come and get her. You should have made someone stay with her at nights when she was by herself. And that poor little girl. She didn't even have that little girl for company any more. No good that. Woman being alone at night. She had nobody. Nobody at all. And you women didn't even lift a finger to help her. Poor little thing left up there now. No mummy or daddy for that one any more. All because of jealous women."

"Look, man. Don't you go around saying anything. Husband or no husband. Mind your lip, what I say."

"Yep, I know poor little thing alright. Kids here say she not too upset when Jipp told her this morning. 'Nother thing. You think I can be goin' around looking after every Tom, Dick or Harry here? How'm I to know she wants to set about killin' herself like that? How'd I know anyone want to do that to themselves? I only *thought* she was like that. Yep, crazy that's what. Lot of people around here like that. Can you blame anyone, hey? I'm askin' you that. Well, don't go around with your big tongue hanging out blaming me. I'm crazy myself — got kids of mine there too in the dormitory. That don't make me happy either. But what can I do? What can anyone do to stop old Jipp and his mob. They run everything here. They in charge. Not me, that's for sure. Do that make me go around wantin' to kill myself or telling other people to kill themselves too? Hey? So shut up your big mouth then. You got too much to say about things you know nothing about."

At that moment Old Donny St Dominic walked into the main camp where the argument was boiling hot about the death of the dead woman. A lot more people were drawn to the action by mid-morning. The main camp was where some of the most influential families lived. The families who truly belonged to this particular piece of country, the traditional elders where the real law of the mission was preserved in strength, in spite of white domination and attempts to destroy it, or to understand what really happens under their white missionary eyes.

The argument progressed into a lot of wrongs, which for some time had been left unsaid, floating around the place.

There were facts to be aired, mostly to do with the inmates' attitudes towards each other. Somehow or other it all became interlinked with the woman's death.

Old Donny St Dominic, about the oldest surviving inmate of those last "wild ones" rounded up and herded like a pack of dingoes into the holding pen, now long pacified, sat unnoticed because of the developing commotion and looked on without speaking.

"You all know nothing!" one old *waragu* or madwoman yells in excitement, racing about excitedly and trying to hit people with her long hunting stick. She laughs hysterically at the top of her voice over the mass argument.

People weave and duck and dogs bark but the debate goes on.

"You the one now who sees things that not even there. Since when you cared about anything around here anyway? No wonder that woman gone now. Praise the good Jesus for taking her, what I say."

"Praise nothing. You churchpeople think nothing. Woman goes and kills herself and no-good Jesus got nothing to do with it. Bloody crawl up fat Jipp's bum — lot of good it will do you."

"Youse know nothing!" the old madwoman yells solidly into

faces, and is told by at least a dozen people to well and truly shut up.

"At least we went to see her and talk to her — tried to settle her down."

"Sure you did. What did you tell her? 'God is going to look after you', did you? God's people take her child away and leave her there crying out like an animal for days afterwards. Only us here had to listen to her all day and half the night. Did whiteman's God hear that?"

"God heard. He heard her. And *you* can't say nothing. I see you down there after Jipp's God when it suits you."

At that moment Old Donny lifts his ancient frame clad in mission rags onto the tip of his walking stick that one of his nephews recently made to support his bulk. Slowly he draws himself into the centre of his balance, then moves one stiff leg after another into the centre of trouble. People watch him approach and stop saying whatever they were saying or about to say about the matter. Silence has fallen all around by the time he reaches the shade of the surrounding young mango trees.

"A woman killed herself here last night," he says quietly, then pauses for a few moments. "Down near Old Maudie's — under the mango tree there."

He stands leaning on his stick and waits before proceeding

any further. "Maudie told me early this morning ... said she been crying again for the child. The one Ivy ... put in the dormitory with the others. Last night ... she come and took Maudie's lighting kerosene ... went and set herself alight."

Someone at that moment put a stool behind the old man and sat him down on it. No one up to this moment had known how the woman had achieved her aim of killing herself. That question had become enmeshed and lost in other issues — the reasons why and who was to take a share of the blame. The method was simply a secondary matter until Old Donny mentioned it: now everyone was dumbfounded, realising how bad the woman must have felt to go and douse herself with Maudie's kerosene then set herself alight.

The old man looked down and waited, thinking someone might want to say something. But the people gathered there either looked at him or down at the ground where the bull ants marched on regardless in their processions from one nest to another and said nothing.

"I went back with Jipp to see Maudie this morning. She's pretty upset, you know. You women here, better look after that old woman."

Maudie was old alright; she looked as old as the land itself. The kids thought she was an evil spirit and would only go near her place to taunt her when their parents weren't around to rowse them. She lived alone, away from the main compound in an old corrugated iron hut and gum tree bower shelter, built by her last husband years ago before he died of smallpox along with several dozen others who fell at that time. Old Maudie never really recovered from his death and preferred to stay in the place alone, too old, or too previously loved and contented to want to share the rest of her life with another man.

The woman who had killed herself had chosen to move into the small abandoned shed beside Maudie's a week after she arrived at the Mission. She was not eligible for a mission hut — corrugated iron, one-room huts that looked like slight enlargements of outdoor dunnies. They were lined up in rows, with a single tap at the end of every second row. One tap for every two hundred people. They housed what mission authorities referred to as "nuclear families". That is, husband and wife with children, no matter how many. If the children had been forcibly removed to the segregated dormitories the couples made room for grandparents, or other extra relatives these people insisted should live with them.

At first Ivy's mother had been placed in the compound of large corrugated iron sheds which housed several families tightly packed together, as well as women alone, with or without children. This was where Ivy had been taken from her. The child was termed a "half-caste" by the mission bosses and therefore could not be left with the others. Their reasoning: "It would be a bad influence on these children. We should be able to save them from their kind. If we succeed we will be able to place them in the outside world to make something of themselves. And they will of course then choose to marry white. Thank goodness. For their children will be whiter and more redeemable in the likeness of God the Father Almighty."

But Ivy was all the woman had left. The child she gave birth to when she was little more than a child herself. The child of a child and the man who said he loved her during the long, hot nights on the sheep station where she had grown up. She had not seen the likes of a mission before. That was a place where bad Aborigines were sent — as she was frequently warned by the station owners who separated her from her family, to be an older playmate-cum-general help for their own children. So she was always careful she made sure to be good. Even to the man who seduced her by night she was good. She believed in love and he loved her just like her bosses did. With kindness.

At the end of the shearing season she was left to give birth alone, as despised as any other "general gin" who disgraced herself by confusing lust for kindness and kindness for love.

Years later, when the child Ivy was half-grown, the woman had to be got rid of. In the eyes of her bosses she was not a bad cook for the shearers. "Now she's had enough practice ... since the time we had to put her out of the house to have her bastard child with her own kind." But the woman was often abusive to everyone. It was said that none of her own people wanted anything to do with her. She was too different, having grown up away from the native compound in the whitefellas' household. And having slept with white men … "That makes black women like that really uppity," they said.

"Now she wants to take her kid with her all the time. Even out in the shearers' camp. Won't leave her even with her own family — after all, she is one of them, isn't she? And the men don't like her either. You know what she went and did? She went and chucked hot fat over one of the fellas when he was just trying to be nice to that child. Caused a right old emergency." A shrug of the shoulders.

"Yes, might have been the father of the child … who knows. Anyway, she's got to go — this sort of thing only gives the others bad habits … if you don't deal with it properly."

A magistrate handled the assault matter and handed the finalisation of the woman's affairs over to the Regional Protector of Aborigines, and she was promptly removed. Under ample protection mother and child were delivered into their new world — an Aboriginal world, a world similar to that occupied by thousands of Aboriginal people at the time. In this case, the destination was St Dominic's Mission in the far North.

When Ivy was taken away, her mother had nothing left. The bad Aborigine became morose. A lost number amongst the lost and condemned, "bad" by the outside world's standards for Blacks. Sentenced to rot for the rest of her days. Even her child taken from her so that the badness of black skin wouldn't rub off.

Her heart stopped dead when they spoke to her just before taking the child, after they had shown her a spot to camp in the squalid stench of the communal shed. It was described as being "for the good of the child." Perhaps they were right — but how could she let Ivy go? She felt her whole body had gone numb. Vanished was any sense of the arrogance of the old days now for Number 976-805 on the state's tally books. Her arms and legs felt as though they had been strapped down with weights.

"No, don't," was all she could think of to say, but the words never passed her lips. Over and over after they left, she thought if only she had said the words out loud, if she had only tried harder, then maybe they would not have taken Ivy away. She had screamed and run after them and tried to drag Ivy away until she was overcome and locked up for a day in the black hole, a place for troublesome blacks. Her release came with a warning of no further interference.

"It is best for you not to be a nuisance. People like you don't make the laws." She was told that next time she would spend a long time inside the lock-up if she still wanted to cause trouble. "And then we will be forced to have you removed to another reserve especially for the likes of people like you. Remember that."

Alone she saw the blackness of the night and the men who came, small and faceless creatures. They slid down the ropes from the stormy skies, lowering their dirty wet bodies until they reached the ground outside the hut while she slept. There in silence they went after her, pulling at her skin, trying to rip her apart. Taunting her as she tried to escape, to get out of the door of the hut. All the while pulling and jabbing her skin wherever they could with their sharp nails. Satisfied with their "bad woman's weakened state" they returned to the skies, beckoning her to come with them. Again and again they came back through the nights to enjoy another attack. Again and again they made her theirs nightly. But her final nightmare was to come.

Alone she can see the black bird fly in the night. See it hover, flap its wings faster to stay in one spot, swoop almost to touch the ground, then shoot up again to its hovering position. The process is repeated several times while the woman slinks into the darkness of the tree shadows. Frightened, on guard, she

105

watches. Now the black bird has time for torment. It attacks in the darkness in the perfect moment — the moment of loss. Its attack is unrelenting. Face, back of head, shielding arms — the pecking persists as she crawls on her stomach into the shack which offers entrapment but no escape.

Hearing the screams, Old Maudie grabs her stick and hits the ground, over and over to frighten what she thinks must be a snake, while she finds her way through the darkness. She hears the flapping of the bird's wings and waves her stick frantically this way and that, striking air, twigs, branches, but the bird escapes. The frightened old woman finds only the terrified, incoherent victim bleeding and shaking, huddled on the ground.

Maudie told Jipp and Old Donny the woman knew she was being punished and would die soon. If anyone could believe Maudie. She knew a lot of stories like that. She said she told the woman not to go on like that, she was young, she should be thinking of finding a husband for herself and having more children. Only old people like Maudie herself thought about dying. But the woman kept saying: "I sick … I sick … sick." That's all she could say. She thought someone wanted her dead. She was a bad woman. Bad mother. Might be someone from her own country wanted her dead and came here secretly in the night to do bad business on her.

That's why Maudie said she did it. Poured the kerosene over herself before anyone could stop her. Before the clouds broke she threw herself in the fire. All the screaming when it finally came, and, by the time Old Maudie could get to the human fireball, it was over. Maudie said she tried to limp over to the mission house to get help for the woman, with only her lamp to see by in the moonless night. Then the rain came. But no one would answer the door there. Seems that as usual, white-man's law did not want to know what happens in the middle of the night. Such are the spirits that haunt the night in Aboriginal places.

"Maudie came and got me to go with her in the night then ... nobody else to do it," Donny said, picking up the story. "Old Maudie and me sat all night long with her ... all night ... you savvy ... in the rain. But it did no good ..."

He looked up and waited for the silence to be broken. But all eyes looked at his and said nothing. Then he said: "That's all." Meaning end of story. The people left and went home.

BLACK LIFE

JACK DAVIS

i am

I am an Aboriginal
I am a city dweller
My dreaming place
is a public hospital
I am an anachronism
My umbilical cord
was severed with a scalpel
tied and sterilized
With surgical dressing
My name is english
But I know my roots
my tribe my skin name
I am irrefutably
indisputably
proudly Aboriginal

black life

The howl of a dingo
Holden or Valiant
Talkin in lingo
That's life

Gettin security
Social I mean
Just out of puberty
jacket and jeans
My life

Knowing who friends are
enemies too
Uniforms uniforms
jackets of blue
Scum life

Gotta listen to music
gotta listen to song
sick of listening to people
saying I'm wrong
Crap life

Lethargic at sunrise
alive after dark
hauntin the fun dives
for a joint and a lark
Dream life

Blood in my nostrils
a nightmare afloat
a mosaic of meaning
caught in my throat
Black life

earth people

Blacks in South Africa are clumsy
they fall off balconies
out of windows
tumble down stairs
maybe they don't like tall buildings
They are earth people

Blacks in Australia
have strange habits also
Such as climbing up walls
with singlet or sock
Or perhaps they don't like the symmetrical
precision of iron bars
They too are earth people

Or perhaps the reason is
or could it possibly be
could be?
No no white man
you tell me

my mother the land

Mother why don't you enfold me
as you used to in the long time ago
your morning breath
was sweetness to my soul
The daily scent of woodsmoke
was a benediction in the air
The coolness when you
wore your cloak of green
after the rain was mine
all mine to cherish and survey
Then the other came
and ripped the soil
and plagued our hearts
yours and mine
The benediction became a curse
of cloven hooves
whip chain and gun
The sun became to me a blood red orb
Nails and flesh fell away
leaving only
whitening bones bare in the summer sun

My voice cries thinly in the dark of night
mother oh mother
why don't you enfold me
as you used to, in the long long ago

the weaving

What words shall I weave today
the joyous sounds of children
the sibilant breeze of summer
the calling of cicadas
Magpies' song of morning
an orange sun at sunset
and in the setting
sending pathways
across the ceiling of the sky

No, I'll tell the truth of falling steel
of women hiding children
in the darkness of their hair
an air raid's wailing warning sound
slicing through the air
Of the flush of sullen cloud
forming shroud on shroud
and of hate that radiates
pain, for all to bear

the writers

They say
we are the makers of history
we inspire others
to laugh to cry and to kill
They say
we are the sages
we write the pages
and out of the figment
of what they imagine
men come steel clad
over the brow of the hill

HOME

LARISSA BEHRENDT

home

"You are a lucky girl, Elizabeth. You have been given a chance, a chance for a better life." The train clicked on. Mrs Carlyle looked out the window again for a moment before returning her stare to the teenaged girl whose head was bent down toward her shiny new shoes.

"*Look* at me when I speak to you, Elizabeth." The girl lifted her face and looked across into the blue eyes. She had been taught to look away when an older person addressed her. But then, Garibooli realised, Mrs Carlyle was not Eualeyai or Kamillaroi so it must be different for her. She looked at Mrs Carlyle's sky-coloured eyes, noticed the wrinkles that danced around her tightly-wound mouth and the thin layer of powder that clung to her skin.

"You must do *exactly* as you are told in the house and do *everything* that the housekeeper tells you. *Without* complaint. And as *best* you can. The Howards were very kind to let you stay with them and earn your keep so you *must* do everything you're asked. Do you *understand?* And from now on, your name is *Elizabeth*, and Elizabeth *only*."

Elizabeth — once Garibooli, now Elizabeth, and Elizabeth only — nodded, too fearful to ask the one question, the only question that mattered to her: when was she going home?

It was in the early hours of the morning when Elizabeth stepped off the train onto the platform with the lettering PARKES framed in the lamp's glow.

They were met by a warm-looking, fleshy young woman wearing a brown felt hat. Elizabeth felt a surge of relief at the sight of the kindly butter-coloured woman, a contrast to the steeliness of Mrs Carlyle. This was Miss Grainger, the house-keeper.

Mrs Carlyle peered sternly into the young girl's face, "Remember what we spoke about on the train, about you *behaving* and doing your best. Miss Grainger here will look after you but you must be obedient and *respectful* to both Miss Grainger and Mrs Howard. Do you understand, *Elizabeth?*"

The girl nodded, even though there was very little she understood as to why she was here, sent so far away, to be with Miss Grainger in the unknown home of Mr and Mrs Howard.

The house was dark against the early morning sky. Massive and ornate, even in the dim light, it looked mythical. Elizabeth and Miss Grainger entered through the back door and, in the flickering candle light, Elizabeth was shown to her room, just off from the kitchen. "You will sleep in here," Miss Grainger pointed to a thin mattress on a wooden bed frame with a blanket at the end. "We'll make some curtains and things and fix this little nook up, and it will look much more homely."

Elizabeth didn't quite know what Miss Grainger was talking about, but recognised kindness in her voice. She sensed pity in Miss Grainger, somewhere in her soft, chubby flesh and her subtle scent of lilac and flour. Elizabeth's "Thank you, Miss Grainger" was for the tone in her voice and the tenderness in her eyes.

Miss Grainger showed Elizabeth the clothes hanging in the closet — two black dresses, two white aprons, two white caps, and a calico nightdress — then left her to settle in.

Elizabeth had cried so much she didn't think she could cry again. She laid down on the bed, alone now, and looked up at the low sloping ceiling and thought about everything that had happened. It was only two nights ago since she was listening to the stories of old Kooradgie, looking up at the Mea-Mei, her head in her mother's lap. She closed her eyes and tears slid down her face. She imagined the world as it looked from up in her tree and saw below the figure of her baina tending the campfire. She heard her brother Euroke call her name. She saw his face, getting smaller and smaller as she was carried faster and faster, further and further away. Then she saw his face again, this time larger. It was still distorted, but with laughter, as she wrestled and tickled him, teasing that he would get eaten by a big fish.

My name is Garibooli. Whisper it. Whisper it over and over again.

The inside of the Howard's house on Church Street fascinated Elizabeth with its polished wood, sparkling glass and gas lights. It offered a thousand curiosities in the shiny silverware and crystal that danced in the light and in the fine china plates that seemed to be the same white colour as Mrs Carlyle. The dining room was a mysterious place with heavily embroidered chairs, garland-patterned rugs and a long teak table. Heavy gold framed pictures of stern men with whiskers and women in stiff, starched garments hung on the walls. Light refracted off every shiny surface. What Elizabeth loved most was the dark wood dining room table's centre-piece: its silver vine with silver leaves holding candles and real flowers. When the candles were lit, glass and gold in the room would radiate and she would be hypnotised, her eyes darting to catch every escaping sparkle.

Miss Grainger, plump and neat, her ginger hair tied back into her cap, ensured that most of Elizabeth's time in the kitchen was spent usefully and efficiently. Elizabeth's day was more than thirteen long hours of hard work and meant meeting the demands of everyone in the house, from Mrs Howard and Miss Grainger down. She worked from six in the morning until ten at night, with a half hour for meals and an hour and a half off in the afternoon. This was intended for free time but instead she seemed to be required to do needlework then. There was a hierarchy of servants, Elizabeth was on the bottom and Miss Grainger, as the Housekeeper, was at the top. Other girls from the town were employed in the Howard house but only Elizabeth and Miss Grainger lived there. Elizabeth often found herself at the receiving end of the teasing of the casual staff, to be saved only when Miss Grainger intervened. Keeping Elizabeth in her place was a role jealously maintained by the Housekeeper.

Elizabeth's work was to be that of a kitchen maid, Miss Grainger told her, but she would also do some duties of a housemaid, such as sweeping the rugs, washing the linen and the interminable dusting. Her first duty of the morning was to clean out the large stove before the cook arrived. She couldn't tend to the ashes without thinking of the fires of the camps. She would be reminded, as she brushed the hearth and arranged freshly cut wood, of the way her mother would stroke her hair, the strength of her father's hands, the way Euroke would lead all the younger boys off to fish, her aunt's soft singing and Kooradgie's stories. She would think of all these glimpses of the life she wanted to return to, before turning her mind to the life she now had.

Elizabeth was to receive sixpence a week pocket money; Miss Grainger would dispense it on Fridays, except for the times when Elizabeth broke a dish or damaged her uniform. She lived on secret hopes that some affection may be shown her by Miss Grainger and, that if she were good, if she did as she were told, she would get to see her parents and her brother again. Obedience and respect, instructed Miss Grainger, were important qualities in domestic servants. Elizabeth was advised to model herself after Christ, the Suffering Servant, and sacrifice her own interests without complaint for those of Mr and Mrs Howard. The lessons from the Bible would remind her of the ways the Reverend who lived near Dungalea Station would preach at her and the other children. The memory of those sermons brought back images of the land she had left behind, the place where the rivers meet.

Running day and night. Never stopping to catch my breath.
But without the wind in my face.
Without the grasses against my legs.
Without the soil under my feet.
Without the pleasure to move free.

Elizabeth slowly became accustomed to the new world of the house; she came to understand its rhythm and pace, its rules and routines. She was not allowed to enter the house through the front door and she was not allowed to speak to the trades-men who came to do work at the house. When Peter, the boy who delivered the mail, came he would try to make jokes with Elizabeth to make her grin. "There's a lot of letters here for you," he would wink, "you must be real popular." He would smile at her and his face, with crooked nose, would transform and seem almost handsome. Elizabeth couldn't keep from giggling.

"Watch him," Miss Grainger would caution. "He's a Catho-lic," she would add, as if that were enough said. Despite this stern warning, Elizabeth was always glad when she was the one to receive the mail.

Elizabeth observed closely and learned quickly. If Miss Grainger told her the proper way to iron a shirt or instructed her to make the tea a certain way, she would do her best to make sure that she did what she was told. It was a reward to her when Miss Grainger would study what she had done and announce, "Yes, that's right. Good."

Miss Grainger was her only ally in the house. It was only when Miss Grainger's own frustrations ran high that she would scold and smack Elizabeth, though remorse and generosity with pocket money followed any cross outburst. Elizabeth came to notice that Miss Grainger's mood swings usually occurred when Mrs Howard was at her worst; it was then that Miss Grainger would withdraw her kind words into a sullenness that would not lift easily.

Elizabeth also learnt to avoid Mrs Howard, who was uncivil towards her with a briskness that shook her youthful sensitivities. Just as Miss Grainger's comments about how good her work was felt like a pat on the head, Mrs Howard's indifference to her seemed to smother that feeling. When cleaning or dusting in a room that Mrs Howard was in, Elizabeth would fuss and work harder in the hope of being noticed. This only seemed to backfire with the response, usually a frustrated, "Come back and do that later."

The girl noticed that Mrs Howard was bitingly curt if her husband had just left, had just arrived or was about to leave. Elizabeth had been curious yet frightened of Mrs Howard from their first meeting but she was also intrigued by the fine bone features and luminous skin with soft trails of veins, like a fragile flower-petal. She was fascinated by the silky flowing flower-bed cloth that hung softly over Mrs Howard's twig like figure. Elizabeth had been surprised to learn that Mrs Howard was not much older than Miss Grainger yet seemed to be made from a totally different material. For Elizabeth it was easy to understand; everyone at home was descended from a certain animal. Elizabeth was dinewan, emu, and so was her mother. But her father was biggibilla, echidna. Elizabeth thought, even though she was white, that Miss Grainger was like a rabbit and Mr Howard was like a fox and Peter was like a camp dog and Mrs Carlyle like a sheep. Mrs Howard didn't seem to be made from any thing. It was as though she had come from thin air.

But it was Mr Howard's presence that filled Elizabeth with an anxious anticipation. He was tall and muscular, with tawny features and eyes a colour Elizabeth had never seen before, the stagnant green of slow moving water. They would sweep past her, sparingly acknowledging her, she could have been painted into the fine floral wallpaper. She somehow felt that it was safer that way. Like Miss Grainger, her eyes would follow his figure as he moved past, though Miss Grainger's stare lingered.

Elizabeth had little chance to explore the town, except when doing errands for Miss Grainger. At those times, she enjoyed the walk past the banks, stock companies, and hotels housed in wattle and daub with corrugated iron roofs and plaster surfaces ruled to give the impression of masonry or bricks.

She was, on occasion, sent to the Chinaman's store for some last minute provision, forgotten or newly needed. She felt deeply anxious when face to face with the Chinese shopkeeper. His abrupt speech sounded like a barked order.

Elizabeth would not have been nearly as brave had the shop owner's daughter not been there. Behind the crowded rows of food, the large canvas bags of flour, the large crates of oils and the tins of tea the girls would talk timidly.

"You are new here," the Chinese girl said to her on Elizabeth's first unaccompanied trip to the store.

"Yes, I'm at the Howard's house. I work there."

"It is so big. What is it like inside?"

"Well, there are lots of glass and shiny things. A big chandelier and the biggest table decoration you ever saw."

"You are lucky to live there."

"Well, the part I live in is like one of those crates over there. And all those fancy lights and ornaments, they just make for more dusting."

The girls' tentative giggles quickly escalated to laughter.

"The Chinese girl" had two names, Elizabeth would learn. She was "Helen Chan" for white people but was born "Chan Xiao-ying." Helen's secret name was like music. Xiao-ying, like a soft breath, was much more fascinating than Helen, just as "Garibooli" was to "Elizabeth". The language Xiao-ying spoke with her father was Cantonese. When he spoke in the language of his people, his voice softened.

The physical difference between Xiao-ying's family and her own fascinated Elizabeth. They were as unlike Mrs Carlyle, Mrs Howard and Miss Grainger as her own mother and aunts were but still Xiao-ying's family were nothing like her own. One time, screened behind the shop's crowded stock, Elizabeth had touched Xiao-ying's eyes; their shape captivated her, the skin around them pulling them tight, making them the shape of gum leaves. In response, the Chinese girl felt Elizabeth's skin, rubbing it softly, giving her forearm a buttery caress. Their differences, under their fingertips, became tangible and binding.

"Where do you come from?" Xiao-ying had asked her.

"Away. My family lives far away from here in the place where the rivers meet," Elizabeth explained as clearly as she herself could understand it.

"Did they not want you?" Xiao-ying asked, her voice low and her eyes to the ground.

"They made me leave," Elizabeth answered, realising as she spoke that she had not made it clear who "they" were.

The young girl's fingers fumbled to unclasp a small brooch. She placed it in Elizabeth's calloused palm and wrapped Elizabeth's cold fingers around the small gift. It was all she could think to give a girl who no one wanted, a girl who caused a flood of feeling inside her, which Xiao-ying hoped could be relieved through this tiny gesture.

Elizabeth studied the carvings in the deep green jewellery that looked like a flower shedding its petals. She felt the coolness of the stone on her fingertips.

"I've never had anything so pretty before. It is even more beautiful than the things that Mrs Howard has."

Elizabeth was awash with guilt for not having explained herself properly but she did not know how to correct the misleading impression she had given, especially after her new friend had shown her tenderness that she had not been able to elicit from Miss Grainger. She didn't know how to explain that her family — although they loved her — had not been able to stop her from being taken away, and had not come for her, at least not yet.

My name is Garibooli. Whisper it. Whisper it over and over again.

Elizabeth would sit on the back porch in the dark of the late evening and look at the stars. Other nights she would walk out into the endless back garden and lie on the cool grass, her body pressed against the earth, the blanket of sky above her. The stars were scattered in the same patterns as they were where she came from so, she reasoned to herself, she could not be that far away from her family and the camp. The moon hung above her, an incomplete question mark; the Mea-Mei, the seven sisters, twinkling down over her. She could hear Kooradgie, the old man storyteller, his voice rising out of the sounds of the evening.

Wurrannah had returned to the camp and was hungry. He asked his mother for some food but she did not have any. He asked other members of his clan for something to eat, but they had nothing either. Wurrannah was angry and left the camp saying, "I will leave and live with others since my own family is starving me." So he gathered up his weapons and walked off into new country. Wurrannah had travelled a long way until he found a camp. Seven girls were there. They offered him food and invited him to stay and sleep in their camp for the night. They explained that they were sisters, all from the Mea-Mei clan. Their land was a long way away but they had decided to come and look at this new land.

Wurrannah woke the next morning, thanked the sisters for their kindness and pretended to walk off on his travels. Instead, he hid near the camp and watched. (Wurrannah had become lonely on his travels and decided that he would steal a wife.) So he watched the sisters and followed them as they set out with their yam sticks. He watched as they came to some anthills and began digging around them. He watched as the sisters unearthed the ants and enjoyed their feast.

While the sisters were eating, Wurrannah crept up to where the women had left their yam sticks and stole two. After lunch, when the sisters decided to return to their camp, two sisters discovered that their yam sticks were not where they had left them. The other sisters returned to the camp, believing it would not be long until the two found their sticks and would join them. The two sisters searched everywhere. While they were looking through the grass, Wurrannah stuck the two yam sticks in the ground and hid again. When the sisters saw their sticks, they ran towards them and tried to pull them from the ground, where they were firmly wedged. Wurrannah sprang from his hiding spot and grabbed both of them firmly around the waist. They struggled and screamed but their sisters were too far away to hear them. Wurrannah held them tightly.

When the two sisters had calmed down, Wurrannah told them that they were not to be afraid. He was lonely and wanted wives. If they came quietly with him and did as they were told, he would look after them and be good to them. Seeing that they could not escape him, the sisters agreed and followed but they warned Wurrannah that their tribe would come to rescue them. Wurrannah travelled quickly to avoid being caught.

As the weeks passed, the two Mea-Mei women seemed to settle into their life with Wurrannah. When they were alone they talked of their sisters and wondered whether they had returned to the camp to let everyone know that two sisters were missing or whether they had begun to look themselves. The two sisters always knew that they would be rescued.

One day, Wurrannah ordered them to go and get bark from some trees so his fire could burn quicker. They refused, telling him that if they did he would never see them again.

Wurrannah became angry. He wanted his fire to burn quicker. He said to them, "Go and get the bark!"

"But we must not cut bark. If we do, you will never see us again."

"Your talking is not making my fire burn. If you run away, I will catch you and I will beat you."

The two sisters obeyed. Each went to a different tree and as they made the first cut into the bark, each felt her tree getting bigger and bigger, lifting them off the ground. They clung tight as the trees, growing bigger and bigger, lifted them up towards the sky.

Wurranah could not hear the chopping of wood so he went to see what his wives were doing. As he came closer, he saw that the trees were growing larger and larger. He saw his wives, high up in the air, clinging to the trunks. He called to them to come down but they did not answer him. The trees grew so large that they touched the sky, taking the sisters further and further away.

As they reached the sky, their five sisters, who had been searching in the sky for them, called to them, telling them not to be afraid. The five sisters in the sky stretched their hands out to Warranah's two wives and drew them up to live with them in the sky, forever.

Elizabeth took comfort from the story of rescue. Looking at the familiar patterns in the night sky and recalling these stories made her feel as though she were lying only a few feet from her home, as if she could look across and see the fire and the shadows of her family through the trees at the end of the Howard's yard. Maybe, she thought, the train journey took less

time than she had imagined. She had been so afraid, everything was unfamiliar, perhaps it felt longer than it was. A
journey always seems longer the first time it is taken, she
reasoned. After all, walking to the store always seemed to take
more time than it took to walk back. So maybe, she hoped, she
was closer to Euroke, Guni, Baina and Kooradgie and all her
family than she had thought. Her family still Eualeyai. Unlike
her, with an altered name. She thought of them as solid and
unchanging.

My name is Garibooli. Whisper it. Whisper it over and over again.

Sometimes, after the work was finished, late at night, with
limbs numb from tiredness, Elizabeth would spend some time
with Miss Grainger. With this feeling of ambient afterglow,
Elizabeth felt bravest and the older woman felt affection for the
child, more, she reflected, than she ever thought possible for a
little darkie.

Frances Grainger had been of the opinion that the Aborigines were too primitive to be able to adjust to life in the civilised
world. She could remember her father's comments that they
were all dying out. And, before Elizabeth was to arrive at the
house, Mr Howard had explained that the best that could be
done was to rescue the children and try to train them. Reflect-
ing on the way in which Elizabeth always tried so hard to do

her chores exactly the way she was told, Frances had to concede that on this matter, as with all else, Edward Howard had been right. When the young girl seemed to yearn for her family and her home, Frances would reassure her that what was being done was for her own good and that she ought to reconcile herself to having a better life and adjust to the new way of life she now found herself in as best she could.

"I wish I knew when I was going home," Elizabeth would say, as the two sat together on the stone back step.

"You can't always get what you wish for. Sometimes home just doesn't exist anymore." Miss Grainger would offer these observations with such measured sadness that Elizabeth knew that there was sorrow as deep as her own within the woman whose gaze seemed to stare inward rather than out, towards the stars.

Elizabeth reflected quietly as she looked out into the darkness. She felt that wherever her mother was, wherever Euroke was, wherever her father was, wherever her tree and her camp were, there was home.

I am running through the grass.
Running further through the grass.
I can feel it whip against my legs.
I can feel the hot sandy soil beneath my feet.

These rare and reflective moments with Miss Grainger went closest to breaking Elizabeth's loneliness, but any intimacy built up in the late evenings had dissipated by morning when an air of friendly formality would fall between the two once more.

Elizabeth observed the way the adults around her behaved towards each other. She realised that because she was not considered very important in the scheme of things, she was often assumed to be too stupid to see what was really going on. But, she thought, I am smarter than Mrs Howard who did not seem to notice how much Miss Grainger seemed to dislike her, as though she was not able to imagine her with feelings. Elizabeth noted the way Miss Grainger would repeat everything Mr Howard said, magnifying its insight, each time she repeated it. And she saw how, when he was at home, Miss Grainger would make an extra effort with her hair, long and like strings of honey, the prettiest thing about her.

At the end of the day, with the dinner dishes washed and dried, the ironing done, the never-ending darning put away, Elizabeth could fall asleep. Her last thoughts were always of Euroke.

He will come. He will come and rescue me.

When the heart of winter came, Elizabeth found herself overcome with exhaustion. Tired when she awoke, her bones would ache, her eyes struggle to open, until she eventually fell back into bed, limp and lifeless, to be shrouded in deep sleep until, not quite refreshed, she had to rise. She was a sturdy girl, used to her share of the work in the camp. Now in the Howard's house the drudgery and loneliness of a kitchen maid's life and the winter chill highlighted her despair at ever returning home.

All she had was the odd lost word from a distracted Miss Grainger, the sly and shy glances from the men who delivered groceries and wood to the back door, the talk of smiles, when Peter delivered the mail, and the occasional exchange with Xiao-ying.

"Come here," Mr Howard one day said to her in the kitchen, a place where Elizabeth had never seen him venture before. She obeyed, just as she had been taught to do. With him being home more, he had been less distant with her than he had been when she first came to the house. Now that she had settled in, he would watch her as she walked past. He would ask her to come over and take his plate from him as he sat on his own at the big dining table and she would be forced to brush against him. These encounters, brief and so innocent, made her feel nervous but also secretly pleased that Mr Howard was paying attention to her. Once she came upon him in his study when she was dusting and he told her she was a good girl with pretty hair and he had stroked it as he told her she must look after it. He asked how old she was and when she said that she was now almost sixteen, he told her that it was a lovely age to be and that she was very grown up. Elizabeth was pleased that he considered her to be mature and as clever as the others who worked there. Too often in the house she was the lowest in the pecking order; everyone got to tell her what to do. It made her happy that someone would notice that she was clever too, especially if that someone was Mr Howard. Miss Grainger always chattered on about how important Mr Howard was, how he was a real gentleman and then she would go quiet as she floated off into her own thoughts. No one has ever noticed my hair before, Elizabeth would think to herself and make an extra effort to ensure it was neat and pretty, just like Miss Grainger did.

Now in the kitchen, Mr Howard beckoned her and as she moved towards him, he leaned in to her and kissed her on the mouth. At first she liked it, the warm-wet touch of his lips, but as his hands grabbed her sides she stood stiff, frightened. He brushed one hand across her breast, down her side, across the curve of her hip and squeezed her, feeling her under her clothes; his other hand held her hard. He was murmuring as though tasting something sweet and melting. Elizabeth was flushed with quivering relief when he stopped, the initial sensual pleasure was replaced by her anxiety and the unfamiliarity of being so close to a man. Her whole body was alert with it.

He drew back, studied her lips, and whispered, after wiping his fleshy mouth, "Of course, we can't be seen like this, can we?" He turned silently and left the kitchen.

Elizabeth stood immobilised, her body inert, her mind racing with a flushing guilt. She had liked his touch at first; then she had hated it, that feeling against her skin, his taste and his force. She was fearful of his weight crushing against her, afraid of what he would do next. She felt ashamed of how she had felt both attraction and revulsion, both on her skin and in her body.

She ached to tell Miss Grainger but she sensed the older woman's displeasure. She was not even sure how to explain it, what to call it, which words to use or what it meant.

She plunged her hands into the wash basin and splashed water on her face, suddenly aware of how hot she had become. She returned to preparing the dinner, her hands shaking as the knife sliced through dirt-encrusted potatoes. She couldn't even be sure, now that the pot was filling with washed and peeled vegetables, that anything had even really happened, whether Mr Howard had been there at all.

She slipped out after dinner and went to find Xiao-ying. As they lay in the grass, looking at the sky, in a paddock at the back of the town, Elizabeth struggled with wanting to tell her friend about the strange encounter with Mr Howard but she felt a wariness about revealing it, even to her only friend.

"Do you ever think about boys?" she asked instead.

Xiao-ying laughed. "Do you mean like to kiss and cuddle?"

Elizabeth smiled at Xiao-ying's amusement and nodded.

"Well, I do not think that my father would be very welcoming to any man who came to take me out for a walk or something like that. But," she giggled, "I do think that the boy who delivers the mail, Peter, is very handsome. And," she paused with a cheeky grin, "I think you do too."

Elizabeth felt herself blush and this made Xiao-ying laugh even more. The laughter was contagious and Elizabeth lost herself in it. When the laughing subsided Elizabeth said to her friend, "Before I was brought here, my family was still trying to decide who I should be married to. There was one man, but he was taken away by police. Mother said they used to arrange marriages but all the old ways are hard to keep to now and the white people do not like it. Will you marry someone who is Chinese?"

"My parents haven't said so but I think that it is expected."

"Do you find white people good looking or do you like Chinese boys better to look at?"

"I like both. I must like white boys because I think that Peter is very handsome." As she made this last remark, Xiao-ying lapsed once more into fits of laughter. Elizabeth, despite her embarrassment that her secret was not so secret, joined in.

The happiness of spending time with her friend, of teasing and shared wishes made the unsettling encounter with Mr Howard seem far away.

One morning, not long after the announcement that the war was over, Miss Grainger came across Elizabeth hunched over and vomiting on the back verandah. She looked suspiciously at the young girl, noticing the emerging dark circles under her eyes and her skin unnaturally lighter. Upon witnessing the same the next morning, Miss Grainger became concerned. She left Elizabeth curled over on the back steps and went to see Mrs Howard in her morning room. "Excuse me, ma'am," she nervously started.

"Yes," Mrs Howard replied, her eyes trained on her letter to emphasise her displeasure at being interrupted.

"I need to speak with you on a matter of some importance … and delicacy."

Mrs Howard looked up, her expression already communicating deep disapproval.

Miss Grainger continued: "I think the little darkie is … indisposed."

"The kitchen girl?"

Miss Grainger nodded, wondering what other "little darkie" there could be.

"How did this happen?" asked Mrs Howard sharply.

Miss Grainger felt herself blush but was relieved when she realised that Mrs Howard (who was, after all, a married woman) hadn't really meant for her to answer.

Mrs Howard sighed. "Send for Dr Gilcrest."

SKIN PAINTINGS

ELIZABETH HODGSON

1. art gallery

I'm sitting in an exhibition room,
alone,
trying to trace my history through the paintings.
Behind me are bark paintings,
earthy tones connected to me,
dot paintings
track the footsteps of my ancestors.
The contemporary artists
are telling their stories, tracing their own histories.
They are not my stories
but they are part of my culture,
a history we share.
My story has it's own canvas,
it's a skin painting.

Beyond this room
is the sound of excited children.
They tumble into the gallery.
At their teacher's direction
they race up the stairs,
crowding into the room.
Some dash from painting to painting
giving their own interpretations.
Others move more slowly.

2. the exhibition room

Far away, the children are laughing
the bark paintings are drawing me:
this is my memory.

I am very small and alone
the room is poorly lit,
outside others play:
this is where I live,
in a State Home with fifty other children.

In this room is a tall glass cabinet.
The door is locked.
There are snakes in glass jars, insects pinned on boards
old photographs of people and places
postcards of deserts and beaches.
Black dolls with European features, a stuffed baby crocodile:
the collection of a tourist.

I see a reflection of a man's face.
He stands too close,
he speaks with an accent.
The things in this cabinet are his.
The bark paintings hang beside it.
I reach out to touch.
His anger and his hands are quick.
I don't like being one of his dolls.
their eyes follow a path of dots.

They all talk at once about water holes, food sources, animal tracks.
They are learning my culture, the path of the old people.
I look at their eyes, noses, their legs, skin.
A teacher calls them and they hurry away.

Two girls linger by the triptych
in one panel a naked white man menaces a young black girl
in the next, she is lying on the ground, her vagina exposed
her vulva red and swollen. She is dead.
One girl points at the penis — "Oh yuck!"
The other points at the damaged vagina.
They step back grabbing each other's hand.

3. ethnographic collection

He and his wife drive to Alice Springs.
They bring back a slide show of their trip.
The wall is bare; a big blunt nail protrudes.
"This is our friend Jacky."
On the wall is an old black man. He is smiling
his eyes are deep, and dark, white teeth.
"And he is a Christian."
Someone murmurs, "Amen."
The nail on the wall is sticking out of the black man's eye.

4. my father's skin

At thirteen I went to live with a stranger.
He was sober, respectable, employed.
My arm beside his was pale.
I asked him why.
He died before he had time to answer.

lucky little girl

Fair hair, fair skin
lucky little girl,
you'll fit in
easily.

A little princess
singled out
for special attention.

We'll teach you to read and write
salute the flag
honour the Queen.

Soon you'll forget
your family:
the black faces
behind wire fences.

At school you'll learn
a new history
of triumphant peace
over a savage black race.

Don't cry for your mother.
Pray and be grateful
for the love we have given,
you lucky little girl.

a world without music

Mr Cage, can you imagine a life without music?
Can you imagine having your acute hearing
and to never hear a melody, a lullaby, a symphony?
Can you imagine a life without rhythm, beat and tone?

This was the world into which I was born:
a world devoid of music,
a world clattering with the rhythms
and beat of everyday life,
the cacophony of knives, forks, spoons,
the pitch in the smash of china.

The tonal variations found in the clink of beer bottles half drunk,
the swish of a straw broom across wooden floors,
the impatient drumming of fingers on a table,
the cries of injury,
the percussion of daily brawls.

Four years and thirty-three days of andante,
allegro, largo espressivo.
The finale — a crescendo:
a black car, a new house
a life without the sounds of my mother.

the reasons why i will not
say sorry

I will not deliberately
hurt you,
nor steal from you.
I will not cheat you,
nor tell you lies.

I will respect
your feelings,
your loved ones
and your possessions.

But I will not apologise
for your situation
nor your circumstances.
They are your own.

I will not apologise for
the abuses I received
as a child; nor say sorry
for the guilt
of my oppressors.

I will not say sorry
for being tied by
shame, guilt and fear
to white man's religion.
And I am not sorry I left it behind.

I will not apologise
for being an Aboriginal person,
nor apologise for my
mother, my father, my family.

I will not say sorry
for my honesty,
my good or bad
sense of humour,
my ironical outlook on life.

I will not apologise
for my political,
moral and spiritual beliefs.
And I make no apologies
for my successes and failures.

I am an
Indigenous woman
of this country
and I refuse to apologise.

the old, old story

Tell me the old, old story
black stranger, how we
travelled the same road:
the stop signs, red lights,
the give-way signs,
and never met.

Tell me the same old story, Uncle,
of life behind a wire fence,
the hymns, the prayers, the rules,
the rations, the cage.

Tell me the same old story, cousin,
of your release
into the warm embrace
of the booze, the drugs,
the gun, the noose.

Tell me the same old story, sister,
about the shame, the humiliation,
the men, the men, the men,
the diseases, the babies,
the pain, the heartache.

Tell me the same old story, Auntie,
of my mother's pain:
her tears, her screams
her anguish and fears
of her loss, her loss.

Tell me the same old story.
I need to hear it in song, in dance,
in black and white,
in the colours of the land, the sea, the sky
from your lips,
your eyes, your heart.

Sister, brother will you stand
and sing with me that
grand old hymn.
O, for a thousand tongues to sing,
to shout, to yell, to scream
our Land, our survival, our future.
Amen.

UNBRANDED

HERB WHARTON

unbranded

For a while Mulga thought he would work and live in the city, where every morning he watched the crowds swarming like ants out of the railway carriages, rushing to beat a factory siren or some other deadline. But after a few months he decided this life was not for him. On weekends the brightly lit hotel bar, the painted women; on weekdays the rush to work, always watching the clock. It seemed to Mulga that everything in the city was governed by the clock, with the workers always looking out apprehensively for the boss. How unlike the bush, where if someone saw the boss coming, they would sit down and wait for him to arrive and have a yarn with him. Here in the city, the men sat down most of the time, and as soon as the boss came into view they would spring to their feet and begin to look busy.

So Mulga greased his swag straps, packed his port and headed outback once more. And it was soon after his return to the bush, after he'd met up again with Sandy and Bindi and joined them on a big droving trip that they became the owners of an orphaned foal, destined to become known throughout the land as "Comet".

They had taken a mob of cattle from Black Rock station down south. After months on the road, Mulga was left to take the horses back north. During the droving trip, one roan mare, a box-headed clumper type, had given birth to a foal, which was now about three months old. One morning, as Mulga drove the horses along the stock-route, in a sheep station paddock owned by a well known sheep breeder and racehorse owner, he came upon a mare lying on the ground. She was dead, probably bitten by a snake. A foal, a colt, wheeled and whinnied around her body. Mulga inspected the dead mare: plainly one of the thoroughbred brood mares owned by the wealthy cocky. Eventually the foal joined the plant horses, now feeding beside a windmill. As Mulga boiled the billy, he watched the tall, clean-legged, racy looking foal mingle with the herd and start playing with old Roaney's foal. After a while her foal became thirsty and began to suck his mother's milk. Then a strange thing happened. The other foal, hungry after a couple of days without milk, tried to suck the roan mare. At first she aimed a couple of cow-kicks at the strange foal. Then, as Mulga watched, she let both foals drink her milk. The hungry new foal drank greedily, sometimes being kicked or nuzzled away by the mare, but he satisfied his thirst.

Well, Mulga mused to himself, it looks like we got ourselves a racehorse! The colt was a rich red bay foal with a star on his forehead. Mulga, resting on his swag, stared up at the spinning blades of the windmill and noticed the trademark in large black letters: COMET. Then he looked at the foal again and said to himself: "I'll call him 'Comet'." So the foal was named after a windmill on a lonely outback stock-route.

Mulga stayed most of the day around the windmill, then packed up the horses and headed north again. The new foal had by now been firmly adopted by the roan mare and the other foal. That evening, just on sundown, Mulga reached the boundary gate of the big sheep station. With the wire fence now behind him, there was no chance of the foal going back to its dead mother.

When Mulga returned to Red Hills with the horses, they branded the foals before turning them loose in the spell paddock. They decided to leave Comet a stallion. (The other foal was never named but always known simply as "Roaney's foal".) Later, they discovered that the station where Comet was found was the home of some very famous racehorses whose owner was noted for the big bets he placed at outback race meetings. Years later, when Comet started to win races, there was much speculation about his breeding and where he came from. Sandy once tried to register the horse, but when he was asked about Comet's breeding, the only information he could give was: "Sire and dam by the roadside — out of the paddock." This was rejected by the racing officials, so Comet remained unregistered.

From the start Comet seemed to be something special. Learning easily to turn and gallop when chasing cattle, they soon realised how fast he was. Quiet-natured, he became a pet, but from the moment he was broken in and saddled he showed his spirit, throwing Mulga as he bucked around the yard. But he would buck only when he was fresh; as they later discovered, once in hand he was like a kids' pony: they would ride him bareback, slide off over his rump or crawl under his belly without a single kick aimed at them.

When Comet was almost four years old he was prepared for his first race at the big Mulga Downs picnic races, where the big stations from miles around brought their horses to try for the Mulga Cup. The three friends sat around the old table at Red Hills and planned their strategy. They decided that Mulga would train him. Mulga had told them of an episode from his childhood days, how he was paid two bob a week as a stable hand, cleaning out the stalls, raking horse shit, feeding, watering and exercising the horses before and after school. Now those long dirty hours in the stables years ago were going to pay dividends for Mulga and his mates.

As the Mulga Cup drew nearer and Comet became fitter, Mulga would go to town some weekends. He would drink and listen to the yarns of an old retired drover called Dasher — no one seemed to know his real name or where he was born. Dasher claimed he had been on every stock-route in Australia, and would talk of his experiences for hours. One night he told Mulga one of his favourite tales which he claimed was true: the real story of the Min-min light which every bushman claimed to have seen, that mystery light that bobbed and weaved, glimmered and glowed, changing colour, appearing then vanishing as it danced just above the ground, seeming to come closer then fading into the distance. Mulga himself had seen lights at night in outback camps, but had always sought some simple explanation — a car's headlights, perhaps. But then he would realise there were no roads.

Once, in timbered country, he had watched a glittering light appear low in the western sky, appearing to dance and weave as it changed colours from red to green or bluish white, a throbbing pulsating glow. Even after watching it for five minutes he could not be sure whether the light moved behind the trees or not. Then it would be gone, leaving Mulga to wonder whether it was the evening star playing games or the real Min-min light.

Now Mulga and Dasher settled down in a corner of the bar. Taking a pocket-knife and tobacco plug from his pocket, Dasher filled his pipe and lit up. At last Mulga was going to hear the real story of the Min-min light: for Dasher declared the light was no mystery at all to him. Years ago, he and his mate, the cook known as Ten-Eighty, were employed by a drover who started off with the biggest mob of cattle in the world. They started out from the biggest station in the world — it was so far west you had to go past sundown to get there. It was a wild mob of cattle; at the beginning of the trip they rushed every night. However, they were soon tamed by the best stockmen in the world. Dasher, of course, was one of these; he claimed that was how he earned his name — when the cattle rushed at night he was always the first to dash to the lead and swing them around. And it was on this same trip, he said, that "Ten-Eighty" got his name. For his mate Barry, as he was then called, was given the job of cooking for the trip. And before Dasher embarked on his story of the Min-min light, he first related the tale of how Barry became "Ten-Eighty".

After a few weeks on the road, the men complained about Barry's cooking. They fell sick with severe stomach pains and claimed they were being poisoned by the tucker they were forced to eat. At last one night, as the men sat down for supper, they looked into the bedourie oven and refused to eat the mixture they saw, demanding the Boss should sack the cook and hire a new one. Then Barry said: "All right, you bastards, if you don't want my bloody tucker I'll throw it out. The bloody dingoes can eat it." So he carried it about fifty yards away and tipped it out. After a scratch meal of corn beef and soggy damper, the men settled down for the night, reassured by the Boss that another cook would be found.

That night, for some reason, the dingoes seemed to be more numerous, and their howls were pitiful. Next morning, the men saddled their horses, stirred the sleeping cattle and set out from the camp. As they passed the remains of Barry's cooking, they saw four dead dingoes around the mixture and another three dogs wobbling and staggering as they tried to escape, while six more dingoes sat and howled on a ridge a few hundred yards away. Dasher, as he described these events to Mulga, claimed no one had ever heard such a mournful sound in their life. The horse tailor, meanwhile, reached for the gun, for dog scalps were worth two quid apiece in those days. But as he took aim, the Boss yelled out: "Don't shoot! If those poor bastards could eat Barry's tucker and survive, they deserve their freedom!" As the herd headed east and the dingoes on the ridge howled louder, Barry was christened "Ten-Eighty" after 10-80, the most potent poison everyone used to control the dingo. Mulga himself knew this name had stuck to the unfortunate cook, but whether Dasher's story was true, he just did not know.

He also recalled that one time when he was drinking in town with Ten-Eighty, the old cook had told him how Dasher himself had earned his nickname — not for dashing to the lead of stampeding cattle in the night, the cook maintained, but because he was always the first to dash to the safety of the nearest tree when the cattle rushed. Mulga thought of this now, as he waited for Dasher to tell the story of the Min-min light. Meanwhile, he ordered rums and beer chasers. Dasher knocked the ashes from his pipe, refilled it, swallowed the rum in one swig, sipped the beer, then continued his story.

He told of months on the road, dust storms, dry stages, flooded rivers. They kept going east and reached the land of the small cockie stations, with fences everywhere and gates to open all the time. At last, after the biggest and longest cattle droving trip in the world, the cattle were delivered. After delivery of the cattle the horses were turned loose for a few weeks' spell before the long trip home. Dasher and Ten-Eighty had agreed to take the horses back home. Their pockets full of money, they booked into a hotel for a well-earned rest. With the horses safe in a paddock, they settled down for a good old-fashioned spree and for the next few weeks they downed the rum. (At this point Dasher started to talk of the barmaid he almost won, and Mulga wondered if he would ever get to the Min-min light.) He ordered another rum for Dasher, who told of how he wined and dined the barmaid, then discovered she was married with four kids — after her husband had punched him in the mouth and told to keep away.

At last, after weeks on the rum, their money was getting low so Dasher and Ten-Eighty decided to muster the horses and head back out west. Loading the pack bags with some tucker and more bottles of rum, they set off. Neither were in the best of health, both almost pickled with alcohol. Their heads seemed to split with each step the horses took. Each night as they got farther away from the town they downed the rum from the pack bags.

Weeks later they passed through a little town where they again filled the pack bags, mostly with rum. By now they had started to argue about things at night as they sat and drank. Then one night, miles from anywhere as they sat around the fire they realised that for the first time in over a month they had no rum. Drinking black tea which they had to imagine was rum they stared into the fire. Then Dasher looked up and saw a car light coming across the rolling plain ahead. "Some-one's coming!" he told Ten-Eighty. "He might have a drink." A little later they looked up and saw the light still in the same place. "He must have broken down," Dasher said, but Ten-Eighty argued that the bloody light was moving and changing all the time. Even as they looked the light appeared to move, to glitter brightly then fade. Then it began to bob and weave, changing colours. Both men now believed it was the Min-min light they saw. "I wonder what makes it glow and dance?" Ten-Eighty said to Dasher. "It's just over there — why don't we take the night horses and catch the bloody thing? Solve the riddle of the Min-min light once and for all!" So both men, almost in the ding-bats after ages on strong black rum, caught the best night horses in the herd and saddled up.

Ten-Eighty grabbed a rope and fashioned it into a loop, tying one end around his now bulging stomach. Out on the plain the light seemed only yards away. "Come on, let's get the bastard!" Ten-Eighty yelled as he swung the rope and let the night horse have his head. Dasher's eyes seemed to light up as he told of the night chase. For about an hour they galloped and weaved across the plain. The light would be just ahead — then as they urged the horses faster, it would disappear, only to reappear behind them. It faded then grew brighter, shedding its ghostly glow as it bobbed and weaved across the plain. By now the horses were in a lather of sweat and foam. Raving about the tricky bloody light, Ten-Eighty raced on once more as it appeared ahead. With one last effort he threw the rope, in a desperate bid to capture the elusive Min-min light, the riddle that had mystified men for ages. As he tossed the loop he was amazed to feel a tug on the end of the rope. The slack raced through his hands as the horse came to a halt. The rope tightened around his waist: with one mighty tug he was pulled from the saddle. As he hit the ground head-first and was dragged along on his stomach, still clutching the rope, he raised his head above the black dirt, burrs and dry grass, calling: "I've got the bloody bastard! I've got him!" By this time the thing on end of the rope was still. Dasher dismounted and came forward. Ten-Eighty began to pull the rope and the Min-min light towards him as he lay on the ground. Then for a moment the light went out.

Dasher reached forward in the dark and felt something soft. Becoming bolder, he felt a long neck and legs, then a lot of feathers. "I think we've caught and killed a bloody emu, mate!" he yelled to Ten-Eighty, who was still spitting dirt and grass from his mouth as he struggled to his feet.

The mysterious light still glowed, and Dasher reached down to see what it was. Protruding from the emu's arse was a torch! He pulled it out and shone it around. "Bloody good torch," he said, "I wonder how it got there." "Bugger the bloody torch," Ten-Eighty answered, "what sort of batteries are inside it? Don't you realise this bloody light has been glowing for over a hundred years? They have to be the best batteries in the world." Dasher unscrewed the end of the torch. After one hundred years the Min-min light went out. Ten-Eighty, still eager to discover the brand of batteries, struck a match. Lying in the dirt alongside the dead emu were Eveready torch batteries.

At this point Dasher stopped talking and wiped his mouth with his shirt-sleeve as Mulga ordered another rum and beer chaser. Dasher then swore this was the true story of the Min-min; to prove it he had the torch and batteries, which still shone bright when turned on. He also claimed that no more lights were ever seen across that misty hazy plain where the emus roam. Morning mist and haze may still reflect mirages of homestead or windmill, but the Min-min light has never been seen since that night.

Then, as Dasher drank another rum, he told Mulga: "You can have the torch, mate, in exchange for a bottle of O.P. rum." And that was how Mulga became the proud possessor of the best torch in the world. After that, when droving stock and watching the herd at night, he would often look across the plains but never see that bobbing, weaving light that used to come and go. Only occasional car headlamps, campfires glowing afar off, and the evening star, which seemed to pulsate and throb as it changed colours in the wintry evening sky. And

Mulga realised that of late no one seemed to speak of the Min-min ... So maybe Dasher and Ten-Eighty *had* solved the riddle once and for all.

Back at Saltbush Station, Mulga put the finishing touches to Comet's training, and at last the big day arrived when Comet and Mulga headed for Mulga Downs and the races.

All along the dry creek and scattered amongst the mulga and gydgea trees tents were pitched, and alongside them were tethered the racehorses, grass-fed and corn-fed, some tame, others real yang-yangs who would buck or bolt when the rider mounted, perhaps not even making it to the start. The last glimpse the owner might have of one of these horses was as it bolted through the trees after tossing its rider.

Around the makeshift bar crowded owners, stockmen and labourers. A couple of bookies were calling odds. The women, despite the dust and flies, were decked out in the latest fashions, their once shining white shoes covered in dust as the ground turned to red powder from the tramp of many feet.

Mulga met up with Sandy and Mary and Bindi, and they planned their tactics for the race. Bindi, the lightest of the three men, was talked into riding Comet in the Mulga Cup. They had an exercise saddle loaned by old Tom from Saltbush, but no racing colours, so Bindi dressed in stockman's gear, R.M.

Williams riding boots, Levis, and a bright green cowboy shirt, the flashiest one he owned. Then all the jockeys, some in polished boots and shining silks, others, like Bindi, in stockman's gear, headed for the start. As the spectators shouted encouragement to the horses they had backed, the Mulga Cup was off around the graded track. Soon the red cloud of dust that was the field reached the straight, where on the inside of the track some posts and rails had been put up over the last few furlongs, to keep the horses on a straight course for the winning-post. As the field made the slight bend into the straight and the leading horses became recognisable, Mulga, Sandy and Mary gave a loud cheer. A couple of horses racing outside Comet could not make the turn: they went bush straight into the trees. Now Comet was alone, six lengths ahead of the field, most of which was still hidden by the huge red dust cloud. He had won!

That night there was merry-making by the light of a camp-fire. Sandy, Mary, Mulga, Bindi, the Preacher, Jam-Tin and many others danced and sang the night away. And Sandy and Mary asked the Preacher to marry them as soon as the new house was finished at Red Hills. At Mulga Downs that day, Comet won the first of many victories he would have in the Mulga Cup over the years. He was destined to become a famous racehorse and the sire of great stock horses of the future.

LAND WINDOW

JOHN GRAHAM

bigger part of us

Gargantuan grey black shapes of all sorts
empty themselves of rain
The setting sun leaves everything a dull glow
Life puts on its deep and starry mask
Sounds start to trickle here and there more clearly
So clearly they become bigger than life
And while our minds were fumbling with the fear
faces as old as the rocks and trees began to watch us
We might have been lying down in a room
or out in the bush
But wherever we were
our deep and starry masks would watch back through us
Nature would filter back into our senses
an amplified meaning
We face this way and that way
but the sun never left us
and the darkness was always there and still
And when we laughed
the deep, dark and starry mask
became a little more comfortable
Stories and laughter around the fire
helped life put on its bright and spacious mask

daytime again
but wherever we are
we'll soon sit around the fire again
because the sun never really leaves us
and the darkness is always there and still
because we'll always do like the planets do —
sit around the sun and tell stories and laugh
whether we're in the bush or in a room
It is the planets', moon's, sun's and stars' sacred way
It is our mother's, father's, uncle's and aunt's sacred way
The stories and laughter are a bigger part of us
It is a bigger part of us —
the sacred way

the map

The very small
go dancing through space

A silent audience
claps a silent clap

Everything learned
off by heart
doesn't go unnoticed

Dust on your eyelash
and everything on the map

the group heart

Birds woven together

The complete V
the heart revealed

Group direction
the heart of their reality

A journey of each other
of food and home

Each held together
by a spiritual net woven
by the very old

To keep together
the group heart

working on us

One day
an overcast day inside the round of our eyes
will cloud the black wells of our pupils

Until we meet again
we will keep the *song* close to us
we will warm the shadow of your absence
around the fire of *song*
around the warmth of the *song*
we will wait for the star to fall from the sleep
we will know when you're home and you're happy
and that you haven't forgotten us

We relate and participate in the great song
therefore we are
and the song is always working on us
therefore it all is, and always shall be

a living land

It's understandable to look for new energy systems
because the one we've got now
is going nowhere fast
But it's not acceptable to search for such things
at the expense of other people
or the earth

It's understandable to search for the promised land
But not at the expense of the indigenous people
of that land

It's understandable to feel confused, hateful, inferior
and desperate in these uncertain times
But it's not acceptable
to keep on letting the disharmony consume you
to keep on letting the learned racist attitudes
cut you off
from the rest of your human family
It's just not right to keep on sabotaging
peace with others

It's understandable to build a future
strong and stable
But not at the expense
of the living children and living land
for life starts with them

And if we are to live forever peaceful
we must speak and demonstrate our will
peacefully
And undo the war on nature
And undo the war on each other
Undo from peace the futureless competition
that does us nothing
and gets us closer to finishing up
with nothing
Better we live together on a living land

portraits

Infinitable light abounce
atomic brush throshing and round
an ocean spray of stars
that only seem more than our own
the bubble thick paint of matter

Clinging gravity threw up our heads
for relative beauty amongst the scenery
the bubble thick paint of matter

Histories mix and views dry
and then the paint cracks
to the sound of bark falling
to the rhythm of others growing

Infinitable light and
eternal cool of the shadow
grow our portraits amongst other portraits
with the bubble thick paint of matter

and let us re-meet
on the canvas of circles
spirit and matter

she said

She said
"Why do you use guns and implements of destruction
    when already the land sings love songs
    to your blood and bones,
    when already
    the spirit knows the holes when you speak
    when already
    the spirit knows the bridges when you're quiet."

She said
"There is nowhere else
    but towards my ocean of milk
    And when you find land
    there is nothing else
    but your relationship with my heart."

HER SISTER'S EYE

VIVIENNE CLEVEN

her sister's eye

She reaches for the butcher's knife, then looks across at Doris. 'You sure you can stand this?'

Doris sits down on an empty kerosene tin. 'Hmm, reckon I can.'

'This one here has got some sorta disease. When you got one bad one in with the rest of the mob, it's no good. The thing is, it infects all the rest. Bad blood, ya see.'

Nana brings the knife back and swiftly runs it deep, across the hen's throat. A stream of warm blood spurts forth. She lays the carcass on the ground and it bucks and shudders as though still alive. Its silly eyes glaze over, then it lays stiff and still.

Nana stands back and looks down at the hen. 'Cos all its chickens were infected too. Same disease. It passed it on to its littlens. Ain't no real good. Had to kill all the chicks. To think, she were one of me favourites, that poor ol girl. Suppose I can always see Treacle Simpson bout getting another one, eh.' She pulls out an empty flour tin from under the tank stand and drags it across to sit down beside Doris.

'Speaking of Treacle, how is he? Haven't seen him for a while.' Doris has an eye still on the dead hen.

'He's good. He's been working across the other side of the river. Building fences for old man Cleaver. You'd have thought Cleaver woulda fixed them fences long before now.'

'Down near the river road, eh.' Doris watches as a swarm of flies blankets the hen's carcass.

'Why, I remember when his father, Joseph, first bought that property. One time there, this was Ruby Midday's boy, Paddy, he used to walk in from the old dump way there. Back then, most us fellahs camped there in tents n humpies. Weren't allowed in town here, except to get tucker then get out again. The copper, Berne Lloyd, would be right on our backsides! Walk behind us to make sure we leave when we finished. Were like we lived in the world's largest prison, eh!' Nana laughs, but it doesn't reach her eyes.

Doris is curious. 'I thought Dave Warner's father was the cop back then?'

'See, this where people get their stories mixed. Weren't never any Warners in this town till later on in the piece. Dave Warner only came here in the seventies or thereabouts. So he's really a stranger. A lot of people forget. See, they *think* Warner a

Mundra boy born n bred but the older ones know better. Most people round these parts are Mundra since generations.'

Doris watches her warily, wondering if she should bring up the subject of history again. She risks it. 'Nana, what about us mob?'

For a few moments Nana scrutinises her. Finally she says, 'Don't count. Never counted then, don't count now. I thought a lot bout what ya said to me the other day and I believe it's true. People need to know their history, otherwise there's this terrible feeling of being lost. There's things I know that may hurt ya real bad, Doris …' She leaves off and looks across to the riverbank. 'But the time has come.'

Doris feels a sense of dread but also elation. After all this time she's going to find out the truth.

Nana begins, 'Now, the Midday boy, Paddy, used to go fishing on the riverbank. Loved old Cleaver's place, he did. Now here's the thing: Paddy used to have this little hessian bag he carried round, kept the snake in it. Can't recall what sort it were but I know it were poisonous. Never saw anyone handle a snake the way Paddy could. Can't say any of us mob were scared of it but Ruby'd be always rousing on him that one day it'll kill him, aye. Paddy loved that snake. Well, on the day Paddy went down there, Joseph Cleaver were standing on the bank with a shotgun. Waiting for that littlen to turn up. When he got there Paddy were hunted off like a dog.

'Now, Ruby were a woman who could get mighty riled! I see her leave the camp that day, Paddy with her. Later on, Treacle Simpson's father, Gus, told me about it. Ruby had an argument with Cleaver and it seems Joseph told her that they were all *trespassing*! Claimed it were all his river n all …'

'The river! He claimed to own the river.' Anger ripples Doris's face.

'As things go, Paddy was terrified of Cleaver. Aye, wouldn't go nowhere near that river. Then, on the anniversary that Cleaver bought the property, the thing happened. Chopping wood, he were, when a snake slithered out of the blocks and got him on the ankle. Later that day he died.'

Doris throws her an incredulous look. 'The boy taught the snake to *kill* him?'

Nana pauses, as though searching for a reasonable explanation. 'No, don't reckon even Paddy could have done that. You see, it was much later that something else happened. Yes, that old camp brought a lot a things out in fellahs. Young Paddy were one.

'Fellahs gotta have roots and at that time we didn't know what he was! Like some of us didn't even know where we came from! Such a thing …'

A flock of crows lands on the fence, eyeing the hen's carcass. They remind Doris of sable-coated men at a funeral.

It's like you feel bad about being black so you try to forget everything. Some fellahs did. Ya ask em where they came from. They say they can't remember. Like their minds were washed away. So what I want to say is fellahs looked to other things. Young Paddy with the snake, for one. It were that snake that gave him something back. Made him feel all right bout who he were.' Nana's wizened, leathery face has a far-away look.

'I don't think it's stupid, Nana. I just don't know what youse went through here.'

'Right, to get back to the story. One day Paddy went missing. We didn't realise at first that he were even gone. It were like him to go round the camp so quiet. Ruby looked for that kid high and low but she couldn't find him.

'It was Gus Simpson who found him … What happened to Paddy I'll never really know. When Gus found his little body it were caught in the roots up the side of the bank. It seemed that when he went in to unhook his line he got his feet caught up. The more Paddy moved, the more he got stuck. Eventually, he musta tried to go under and untangle the line. All the while that snake bag were on the bank, just out of reach. What happened next is anybody's guess. The *thing* is, while Paddy was drowning, the snake got out of the bag! It were later on when Gus found the marks on his arms. The snake had bit him! I can't pretend to know anything much about it, but I know this much: *that snake killed Paddy before he drowned.*'

Nana halts for a moment and catches her breath. 'As I said, there ain't a great deal I can answer about it. I reckon it goes back to that kid having something with the snake. Aye, in times of strife there's magic in a lot a things. Like a strong hope, or a love that can't be held down. What do I reckon happened? Well, the way we were treated out there on the old dump road, anything coulda happened to anybody. Young Paddy was trying to take part of that river as his own place. It was much later, when the other thing happened with Belle Gee …' The old woman stops, her milky eyes straining. She looks off towards the river. Memories and grief wash over her face. She hunches forward, hands between her legs as she peers off into some remote place.

From the end of the street a horse trots into view. It stops on the dusty road and raises its pretty sorrel head. Its smooth chestnut coat ripples as flies swarm its rump.

A gust blows in from the west. Leaves and paper scurry about in a dusty dance as the breeze gathers force and with a quick swoop it lunges over the carcass of the hen. The horse's nostrils quiver and it throws its head back with a sharp, bone-cracking jolt. Blood-mad from the scent of the dead hen, it rears, pawing and slicing the air. Red soil cuts through the air as it bolts down the road.

'They hate the smell of blood.' Nana goes over to the carcass and lifts the bloodied hen. 'Reckon we oughtta bury this poor creature, eh.'

The soil breaks away easily as Doris digs into the dirt. She takes the hen from Nana and lays it in the hole. 'Do you think that's deep enough?'

'Yes, my girl,' Nana answers, looking into the hole with a frown. 'It seems the dirt ain't what it used to be, either. I can't grow anything much in the yard now. That's why I have to plant the chrysanthemums in those tubs over there. Aye, the ground just won't give.

'Okay, Doris, let's have a cuppa, love. Then I'll tell ya the rest of the story.'

Nana brings her head up. 'I must go on with the story, Doris. It's comin to me, clear.'

'Nana, ya really don't have to.'

Nana seems not to hear, she slips back into memory. 'It's Sunday, a hot day, so hot the ground burns the soles of ya feet. I'm hanging out the washing and happen to look over at the river. I think I see someone on the other side. Where the

Cleaver's property is. I make out a shadow movin through the bushes, movin very fast. It just don't *look right* …'

'Nana?' Doris quizzes.

'Before I go much farther, go switch the wash-room light on, Doris. It'll be dark soon and I don't like the darkness. Pull that drum over closer to me, Doris,' Nana motions. 'Alright, here goes. The shape's movin fast. I turn to see if anyone else is about, but most of em are down on the riverbank swimming n fishing. I spot Mertyl Salte close by, stirrin the billy tea. "Mertyl, over here, look," I yell. She joins me at the line and looks over at where I point.

"I'd say, Vida, that's Tom Cleaver over there." Thinkin she was right, I don't worry about it too much; after all, Cleaver spying ain't nothin new. I walk back to me tent when I notice some of the fellahs have come back from fishing. Joe and Lilly have caught some cod and are gutting them on the ground. A few minutes later Mertyl comes back ta join me as I stand countin how many fish be caught. Suddenly there's a loud bang! First I think it were a car backfiring up the dirt road. But a terrible feeling tells me that it were a gun. No one panics; after all, people shoot pigs and roos down near the river. Then Mertyl says, "Don't feel right. I don't like this, Vida. Where's everybody?' Someone pipes up, 'We're all here, except for Lilly's littlens.' Everybody freezes. All eyes turn ta Joe and Lilly.

Lilly's mouth drops wide and she places a hand over her heart. "No," she whispers …'

Doris feels her whole body break into a tremble. 'No, Nana, no!' Her mouth tastes coppery, she tastes her own fear.

'Do you want me to go on, love?'

Doris sucks in a large breath. 'Yeah, Nana, go on.'

'Mertyl Salte is the first to break from the group. She gallops down the riverbank, me tearin after her. We reach the lower part of the bank. And there she were, laying against the trunk of a ghostgum. She looks like a red n white flower. She has on this pretty white frock, Lilly sewed it by hand. A red spot, like an ink stain, spreads all over the front a her dress.'

Doris shuts her eyes tight. *Smack bang in the heart.* The vivid image plays in her mind. She wrings her hands into a fierce painful knot. But still she listens as Nana goes on.

Nana's voice is now low and whispery. 'And there's Raymond, alive, holdin his sister's hands, wailin. He's only a twelve-year-old child. But Belle's still alive, barely. As she lay dying, her last words be: 'Raymond, help me …''

Doris feels the shift in the now shivery night air. Her eyes fix on Nana.

A small wail escapes the old woman's mouth. She stands uneasily to her feet, shaking a frail fist up into the darkness. She stumbles against the tank-stand. Doris shoots forward, grabbing her by the arm before she falls. She gathers Nana into her arms. 'I'm sorry, Nana. I'm sorry,' she murmurs, hot tears burning the back of her eyes.

'Nana, I'm staying the night.' She leads Nana up the steps and makes for the bedroom. She pulls back the blanket, arranges the pillows and helps her into bed.

Nana crumples amidst the pillows. 'There's more, my girl. That's half the story. You got the power to change things, Doris,' she finishes.

Doris nods. She can't answer. She has lost all power of speech. She turns from the room, goes into the kitchen and looks from the window out into the night. From the end of the road she can see something in the half-light. The horse stands by the undergrowth, seeming to look straight at her. Doris turns away. Suddenly the night feels very lonely.

When she sleeps she dreams of many things.

DREAMING IN URBAN AREAS — COME DANCIN'

LISA BELLEAR

grief

This is not about love or
hurt or hate

This is not about
battery hens, Mcdonald's hamburgers

This is not about
acid rain or conspiracy theories

This is about me
my life, my grief my
need to maintain
the capacity to love.

chops 'n' things

(for Eva Johnson)

I can't wait to curl around
a lemon scented tree
light a fire and
watch it burn down to
the embers as the sun
floats away, far away
our ancestors are
yarning and laughing
at this Koori woman
and through the
flames, the embers
and the burnt chops
and charcoaled
potatoes wrapped in foil
they're saying, tidda girl
you're okay,
keep on dreaming
keep on believing

mother-in-law

Took me thirty years before I left your father
Battered wife syndrome, well that's the term the
Social worker used at the neighbourhood centre
Oh I didn't realise I was being abused. On the bad days
I never left the house, told friends, not that I had many
I was visiting a relative who had taken poorly
Look at me sweetheart, you've made the right decision
Believe me, you have to think of Stacy, and don't forget
You have to take care of yourself. Mothers have rights
Mothers have needs too. I'll not make excuses for
Your behaviour, you have to work through that, nor
Can you say it was all Larry's fault. Honey don't cry
Together we'll be okay, you've got to stop hating yourself
Alright, the court order allows fortnightly access visits
On the proviso he's not been drinking — listen he's not
Doing right by you or Stacy, coming here drunk. He
Hasn't even bothered to shave. Darling, he may still care
He may even still love, but rules are there for the protection
Of the child, and for the sanity of the mother. Maybe the
Next time you will be able to welcome Larry inside but
For now, tonight, the situation, the reality is no, and if

He's still there in five minutes, Larry knows the score
There's a train, or there's a police van
It's up to him

HARD YARDS

MELISSA LUCASHENKO

hard yards

By the time the hearse pulled into the yard of the Chapel, the heat of the day had finally turned to darkness and solid sheeting rain. Hardly anyone had thought to bring umbrellas, so they stood awkwardly under the inadequate protection of the chapel eaves, pretending that they didn't mind getting wet, not with Stanley lying there cold, and Aunty Della King gone pale with the strain. Talk about bad luck, eh. That woman had the worst luck in the world, even for blackfellahs.

Everything had already been pretty much said at the community meeting on Saturday morning. The men clumped together in silence and looked at the ground. Pairs and threes of shattered women spoke softly to each other. (Whose son next? Whose nephew? Which, in ten years, of the baby boys now being nursed in the steamed-up cars by their mothers, whose casual love was today briefly replaced by a close-hugging and a cossetting of the bemused tots; by refusals to pass bubba on to Aunty, or even Nan.) The teenage girls shivered in inappropriate sexy black evening dresses, the rain sliding in silver droplets down their bare arms and backs. Other than Darryl, who was constantly beside his mother, the dazed young men stood on the fringes of the group, their anger building as they smoked and swore. Tonight their families would cop it, and any strangers who carelessly wandered into their orbit. They would punch their love of poor dead Stanley onto the bodies of others. No one could say they didn't care then, no one could ignore them and the horror of their loss. For now though, they cursed the police, the screws, the doctors, the migs, the whole white world. They kicked at grass and car tyres, bowed their heads and folded their arms against the rain.

Just as the coffin had been borne inside, a late arrival, a taxi, pulled up a little away from the group. Roo burst out of the passenger door and walked quickly up to take his place next to Shaleena and Darryl, ignoring the curious looks he got for being both late and white. He gave Darryl a hard angry hug, then leaned across to grasp Jimmy's shoulder, but Jimmy swung away in contempt. Roo knew what he was thinking. The mig again. Who invited this white cunt to Stanley's funeral? Why'd Darryl let Shaleena go with a mig in the first place? Roo stood stockstill. *Let it go.* He didn't really expect anything better, not today of all days. Darryl motioned with his head. Forget it, man, come over here. You'll be right. Roo stood, seething, for a beat of three, then shifted.

"You took ya good time," Shaleena accused him after he'd taken her five-dollar note over to the taxi. "Everyone was asking where ya were. Sayin ya got no respect." Roo shrugged off this invitation to an argument. A series of stress-fractures were running through his life, and he was having to concentrate just so he didn't spin right out, eh. His fingers were doing that tingling shit they did when he was about to spin. Cos Stanley was dead (*dead!*). His probable father was a mean, hard prick who didn't give a shit. Shaleena was always on his fucken case. Behind in his training. Never any money for escaping this life. Roo stared at the length of the shining hearse, blanking out. After a moment Darryl put his arm around Mum's heaving shoulders and then they filed inside, Roo too. White or not, screwup or not, it was time to say goodbye to buddaboy.

Inside, dull rectangles of light showed where the stained-glass windows were being lashed with rain. At the front of the church, Uncle Eddie was conducting some business with a smoking bucket of gum leaves. Mum went to the old man and cried on his shoulder. Then Darryl ushered her along the front row and sat himself down beside her without removing his arm. Rock of Ages. The rest of the family took up the opposite and second aisles, and community members sat in descending order of importance or self-importance behind them. There was little talk, just the sad quiet sound of the congregation brushing rain off themselves and preparing to mourn among their own. Roo had a better grip on himself now, but he could have almost wept when he saw the preacher step up to the front near the altar thing. Fucken hell. The man could talk the leg off an iron pot. Off a *fossilised* pot. No wonder he became a preacher. Well that way he got a captive audience, didn't he? He could talk underwater with a mouth full of wet cement, he could, truegod. Uncle Eddie retreated, taking his bucket outside. His job was finished, for now.

"Dearly beloved," the preacher began, "It has fallen to me on this tragic occasion to say a few words …" And on and on he droned. A few words, Roo thought hysterically after fifteen minutes, more like a few million. After what seemed like a thousand "O Lord"s and ten thousand "Christ in whose name we are redeemed"s, the man drew his sermon to a long and trailing close. He looked up from behind his glasses as if he was about to recall some vital point he'd accidentally failed to cover, but Darryl stalled him by standing and pulling a single sheet of paper from his shirt pocket. He strode up and the preacher, displaced, reluctantly stood aside, hands behind his back.

Tall and stern in a borrowed suit, Darryl looked out over the patchwork of faces, their undivided attention turned back on him. Somewhere stranded in the middle sat three women, two of them white, dressed in the pale blue uniform of the Queensland Police; the seats beside them were glaringly empty. The silence of the crowd held as Darryl fought for composure. He was well-liked, well-respected, by those who knew him, and those who didn't were hushed by the circumstances of Stanley's death and by the name King. Darryl smoothed the paper in front of him on the podium. A lightbulb flashed from the back of the room, prompting a brief angry murmur which subsided as Darryl started the eulogy for his cousinbrother.

"Brisbane Elders," he began strongly. "Visitors from the Kombumerri, Wakawaka, Gabi Gabi, and Muninjali tribes. Minister Jackson, uncles, aunties, brothers 'n sisters, I hafta welcome you here today on behalf of the family. We're here today to say goodbye to … to a special young Murri fella who was took before his time. Our brother, Stanley —" and here Darryl's voice broke into a harsh rasping. He straightened himself up with such obvious physical effort that it turned Roo's heart to water. Others in the audience were pushing back the swelling tears with the back of their hands. Wet faces gleamed in front of the speaker.

He went on. "Stanley used to say that for Murries hard times come easy. Before young brother was taken from us, I used to think that he meant Murries're always getting into trouble, and that it wasn't ever hard for us mob to find hard times. That we didn't have to look too far for em. Now all of us here who knew my brother knew he wasn't no angel. He'd seen the inside of a lockup more than once; he done wrong by some people, including some people here today, and I hope he knew it, too. But Stanley didn't deserve to die the way he did. He was a young one, just a child of seventeen." Darryl paused, and he abandoned the paper in front of him.

"I been thinkin ever since it happened, ya know, thinkin that maybe what Stanley meant when he said that hard times come easy was that when you see enough hard times, you get sorta good at it, if that's not a silly thing to say. How many times've we seen each other at the funerals of young ones, young fellas, this year? And what about last year? Or the year before that? We need to, we need to stick up for each other, not always be knockin each other, or lettin each other just … go. There's too many of us going. We been here too long to give up now … Forty thousand years this ground's been trod by black-fellahs jinung. Fifty thousand! More … You, and you, and you —" Pointing to wide-eyed young men. "You gonna be next? Or you?" Darryl shook his head in sorrow, muttering under his breath that he didn't know, he didn't know. Then he spoke up again.

"Anyway, I don't know much 'bout politics, so I'm not gonna say nothin' much about that side of it. I wanna tell youse about Stanley, anyway that's what we're here for, eh. I wanna remember the good stuff, happy times. One good thing I remember, me 'n Stanley went long last year to that show at South Bank, you know that one from up North with them paintings. We had a bit of a look around at em and then we talked to that old fella that come down from the Cape. He was real quiet, eh, he only said a few words to us, but I never forgot what he said, talkin about his country up there. Said he was real homesick goin away from his people and his sites; his grandfather dreaming was waiting there for him to go back and finish up there. Said it, just like that. He didn't look sick to me, just old, but then about a coupla months later someone told me, sure enough, he went back and passed away there in the first week he was home. He knew. He *knew*. And you know what it was he told us, me and Stanley? He liked Stanley, see, took a shine to 'im cos he was such a deadly didge player, and he said, don't go thinking you lost your country, boy. Said it was still there waiting, said the spirits are all 'round, daytime, night-time, allatime, and they very patient. Two hundred years!" Darryl spat the words in the policewomen's direction. "What's that to fifty, sixty, seventy thousand? Nothin. That old fella he took us over an' showed us somethin in one of them

215

pictures, this crocodile dreaming it was, and he reckons, 'When you know your country proper way, it grows into you, grows through your heart and your blood and then they can't never take it away from you cos there's no difference between it and you.' That's what he said — they can't never take it away." Darryl glared at the crowd.

"That old fella was talking about finishing up and he sounded real happy, you know. I think maybe … maybe he was trying to tell us something that day, maybe he seen more than his own future there. Anyway. He gorn now. Stanley was our brother, our son, and our cousin, and he's gorn too. He part of our country, ere la." Darryl had by now accepted the wetness running down from the corners of his eyes, and his words were punctuated with gasps and sniffs.

"Stanley wouldna been happy 'bout finishin up, specially not this way, but I know one thing, his country's took 'im back. They can hate us, and they can even kill us, but they can't do nothin 'bout that, we belong ere. And so long it's here wif all of us, so's he. Youse wanna remember that when ya hear them white fellahs talk 'bout him on TV and that."

Darryl looked up bleakly and in a gesture that came from nowhere cut the air with his right hand. "Okay, thassall now." He went and sat down again as the preacher organised everyone to sing "Amazing Grace". Tears ran from his tightly shut eyes. Jimmy and Mum King clutched at Darryl from both sides, weeping. Roo reached forward from the row behind and grabbed the man's shoulder with his pale hand. Darryl's hand came back and covered Roo's as the two of them looked down at the floorboards. As his mate sobbed his heart out, it was all Roo could do to stop himself from crying. Yer just a weak cunt, he told himself. But the tears didn't go anywhere in a hurry.

Mum King poured boiling water out of the still-switched-on kettle over her two teabags; not a coffee drinker, she wanted it nice and strong, cos of not sleeping. She plonked the scarred plastic kettle down and flicked the power off at the wall. The kettle subsided with a last aggrieved, breathy whistle. Black like me, Mum thought, as she stirred the bags with a fork, then pressed the last drop from them, making the tea darken, black like me. Me and me boys. Funny the way they all come out. Me dark, and Joe and Frank both fair, Lord bless em, ya'd think it'd be the girls what'd be dark, but it was me boys what all come out black. Lose us in a dark room, ya could, we shut our eyes. Ah, no matter 'bout colours. Only I lost my beautiful dark boys, see. Sadness suddenly welled up in her. She tried to stop counting the loss of Stanley over and over, tried to consign him to that place where John and Trev already were. Lost ones. Too hard. Tears pricked at her eyes.

Mum found the sugar packet and stirred in a heaped spoon-
ful. She hesitated, then added a second, grabbed Leena's
smokes packet and lighter and carried her kit outside to the
steps overlooking the street. A little possie to watch the street
from. Her cup rasped as it met the concrete stair tread, and left
a wet semicircle underneath. Mum lit a cigarette and looked
out at the world of Park Road. Nigga's busy feet had worn a
dusty path in the grass around the house, and as she watched
he came trotting along it to say hello.

"You're a big Doris you are," she told him, wiping her eyes.
"Poor old Nigga …" The dog stood foursquare at the base of
the stairs, panting with love and drool. Dogs now. Jimmy was
the one for dogs. Stanley never did like 'em much, always too
scared, him. Same with Roo, eh? (the little shit). Even with
Nigga, he never really clicked, never trusted him not to turn
and go him. Jimmy slept with the dog, talked to him, did
everything with him, short of that, a course. But not Roo, and
never Stanley.

"Why zat, Nigga?" Mum growled at the animal. "Eh? You
too uptown for 'em, uh? Cos ya white. You'n the parkies' dog,
both whitefellahs you are, sha-ame." Brindle and white, Nigga
stood and panted, impervious to her teasing.

"Which way now? Jimmy gorn out an left ya, has he?"
Nigga cocked his eyes in her direction, understanding every-

thing. Mum sighed, wishing Uncle Eddie was around, but he'd gone bush again. The city was no place for a Lawman, he'd say, and disappear, for a week, or a month. There hadn't been hide nor hair of Uncle to be seen since the funeral.

"C'mere Nig, c'mon," Mum urged, suddenly wanting him close. The dog climbed the stairs heavily, then tossed his head up under Mum's hand for a sook. "There, that's a boy." She rubbed his neck with the side of her hand. Hoping for a crust or crumb, Nigga sniffed at her and finding none turned away in disgust. Down the stairs, back to the dust. Mum snorted. "Ah, garn. Woss the matter with ya? I'll flog you," she threatened as he wallowed in dirt. "Don't think I won't. Ya turn ya big black nose up 't me, ya cunt." Good go, knucklin up to the dog. They'll be lockin me up soon. Mum smiled a tiny sad smile, forgetting to grieve for just an instant. The first moment of forgetting that would stretch, soon, to minutes, then the minutes to hours and the hours to days, until one morning she'd wake and her first heavy thought wouldn't be of Stanley at all, but something, someone, else.

"Nigga," she called as he searched for fleas along his spine. "Nigga!" He turned a lazy eye in her direction, then sprang quickly to his feet, whining and cringing.

"Ah, what now?" Mum asked, exasperated.

Nigga flattened himself onto the grass, looking up to the

open door. Mum turned where she sat. When she looked
behind her, her fingers forgot themselves and she dropped her
cup, strong black tea and all. It shattered on the tread, tea
splashing and running along the concrete grooves, dribbling
into the dust. The broken pieces lay where they fell. In the
doorway stood Stanley in his Broncos shirt. Behind him, Mum
could see the stereo system and TV, and Leena asleep on the
lounge. Facing Mum, Stanley beckoned her inside. His face
bore the same energetic persuasion it had when he was alive, as
if he was saying, *look la! Come see in ere* … Ashen, Mum shook
her head. Stanley frowned and pointed to his shirt. Stains
began spreading across it, a crimson blossoming that soon
covered the white folds. As it spread, Stanley pressed his hands
against his chest, as though trying to stop the flow. A strange,
gurgled lingo rose from his throat.

"Stop it!" Mum ordered him in a stern whisper. "Stop it,
Stanley! You got no call!" On the lounge Leena shifted her
weight and moaned a little.

"You stop it now, boy." Mum said fiercely. "We ain't done
nothin to you, now you go — you hear me? You go back!
There's nothin for ya here now!"

Stanley turned and pointed at Leena. Mum's heart stood
still. No, no, God, no, not another one, please. *No!* Not
another one, no oh no. Dear God.

A rage started within her, a deep, menacing rage of protection for her daughter. "Whatchoo mean? Leena belongs here, with me! With us. You bugger off where you belong, steada trying to frighten an old woman, shame! Gorn — fuck off!"

He began to laugh at that and to move down the stairs. Mum took a step backward and then another. She glanced behind her. Nigga had disappeared. Typical, fucken useless thing like its owner. Leave her in the lurch.

The black woman stood on the front lawn, alone and barefooted, standing in the cup's broken shards and facing the ghost of her baby son. Shaking, she mustered the courage to address Stanley once more.

"Tell me whatcha want then," she pleaded. "I din't mean to call yer name, St … son, I just … gets so lonely at night, thassall. Thassall, I din't mean ta call fer ya to come, not really, I'm sorry if I disturbed ya, boy …"

He stopped on the middle step, shook his head and pointed once more in the direction of his sister.

This time Mum finally understood, and the terror left her. Her tone turned to a mother's counsel. "Ah … okay, okay. I know. I know whatcha mean. I'll make sure. Garn, then. Go back, boy … this no place fer you. We love ya, son, but it's no place …"

Stanley turned and went up the stairs into the house. Mum

221

held her breath, waiting for Leena's shriek, but there was no sound.

"Leena?" she called. Then a bit louder. "Leena?"

A bloodcurdling scream and Mum bounded upstairs. "Wha —" she cried, but Leena was standing in the middle of the lounge and Stanley was gone.

"What is it?" Mum demanded, her eyes fixed closely upon her daughter.

"I dreamed, I dreamed —" Leena was shivering. "I had this nightmare, that Stanley —"

"Now, girl, don't you be saying that name to me. There's been too much talk. No more. No more saying it. That name's not to be mentioned in this house."

Leena gulped, her eyes still frightened. "I dreamed he come back. And he said Roo hadda come back too, and we all hadda live here, with him, with his ghost, here in this house. That we couldn't ever leave, none of us. Never."

"Ah, now, s'just a bad dream, you gotta expect them when yer this way, eh. Nothin unusual there, just being pregnant, thassall, doan worry 'bout it." Mum soothed her. Leena felt like having a go at Mum, but a sudden brightness about her mother held her back. There was something of the old Mum King in the woman facing her. Despair had fallen from Mum's face, and even her newly grey hair couldn't take away the strength in her stance. The girl contented herself with a muttered, "well ya coulda bloody told me" and a fast hard stomp to the loo.

OF MUSE, MEANDERING & MIDNIGHT

SAMUEL WAGAN WATSON

jetty nights

it was an arm that stretched over the mud and sharks
from under the song of the swaying pines in the darkness,
the night water fondles the pylons
as mullet dance in the cold blackness afraid of nothing
we too, walk against our curfew
we see the eyes under the jetty,
phosphorescence and ectoplasm
under the death of the floorboards
looking up from the muddy grave
stealing a glance at the clear cover of stars

a fishing boat drones somewhere out there on the water
and in the distance a buoy flashes red lights and green
and you suddenly feel the loneliness out there
that's where you can escape to

the smell of mashed potatoes and chops hang in the air
drags our attention back to the shoreline cottages
Ray Martin chatters somewhere in the glow of sixty watt lighting

we turn and face the clatter of dead wood
our lifeline home
and leave our jetty,
leave away the mystical squawks of curlew in the swamp
that eerie bleakness we came to love,
this innocence we behold
that we had nothing to fear but our parents' scorn

cheap white-goods at the dreamtime sale

if only the alloy-winged angels could perform better
and lift Uluru; a site with grandeur
the neolithic additive missing from that seventh wonder of the
    world expo,
under the arms of a neon goddess, under the hammer in London,
murderers turning trustees
a possession from a death estate
maybe flogged off to the sweet seduction of yen
to sit in the halls of a Swiss bank
or be paraded around Paris' Left Bank
where the natives believe
that art breathed for the first time;
culture, bohemian and bare and maybe brutal
and how the critics neglect the Rubenesque roundness of a bora-ring
unfolded to an academia of art
yes, that pure soil in front of you
the dealers in Manhattan lay back and vomit
they're the genius behind dot paintings and ochre hand prints
rattling studios from the East Side to the Village
and across the ass of designer jeans
porcelain dolls from Soho wanting a part in it so bad

as the same scene discards their shells upon the catwalks
like in the land of the original Dreaming
comatose totems litter the landscape
bargains and half-truths simmer over authenticity
copyright and copious character assassination on the menu
sacred dances available out of the yellow pages
and
cheap white-goods at the Dreamtime sale!

on the river

it was a drive through the sleeping industrial giants
and thirty minutes before a flight
along Brisbane's vein of union disputes
to a secluded spot on the river's edge
with it's cold sea breezes and dead things,
we kissed
and said goodbye
discovering that we both had feelings for deserted factories
and abandoned mechanical bits
and for each other
thirty minutes before a flight
and two writers can't find the words
to ease the tearing of departure
serenaded by a blow-torch on a rusting iron hulk upon the water
grey smoke billowing from the old power station
the landscape studded with electric fences and weeds
her and I at home amongst it all
we kissed
and said goodbye

chloe in the window box

in the darkness
it's increasingly difficult to find the corkscrew
and Chloe in the window box
with that bottle of pinot noir

or the memory of her
that left six months ago
and light no longer shining through
her window
where as a sentimental act
we clasped and watched the stormbirds
that no longer cross the shoreline
Neptune no longer taunting
peering through his transparent keyhole
no more 2am's
cut out of the darkness with a corkscrew

and as time stretches on
a distorted picture of Chloe,
an empty bottle of pinot noir

white stucco dreaming

sprinkled in the happy dark of my mind
is early childhood and black humour
white stucco dreaming
and a black labrador
an orange and black panel-van
called the 'black banana'
with twenty blackfellas hanging out the back
blasting through the white stucco umbilical
of a working class tribe
front yards studded with old black tyres
that became mutant swans overnight
attacked with a cane knife and a bad white paint job

white stucco dreaming
and snakes that morphed into nylon hoses at the terror
of Mum's scorn
snakes whose cool venom we sprayed onto the white stucco,
temporarily blushing it pink
amid an atmosphere of Saturday morning grass cuttings
and flirtatious melodies of ice-cream trucks
that echoed through little black minds
and sent the labrador insane

chocolate hand prints like dreamtime fraud
laid across white stucco
and mud cakes on the camp stove
that just made Dad see black
no tree safe from treehouse sprawl
and the police cars that crawled up and down the back streets,
peering into our white stucco cocoon
wishing they were with us

BRIDGE OF TRIANGLES

JOHN MUK MUK BURKE

bridge of triangles

Way back then Spring arrived, Mick arrived and the floods arrived.

Sissy and Mick were off at one of their sessions in the Empire. Jack was doing some casual work at some place or other. The sky was low and roaring, yellow and sinister. Shirl was looking after the six kids. Joe and little Mary had not been to school since their mother had taken off with Mick.

The wind whipped through the long polished grass and the children sensed the electric tension in the air. It was quite dark at about three in the afternoon. Shirl's toothless mouth was tight. Her deep set eyes kept scanning the sky and her forehead crinkled. Every now and then she would wander off to look at the river. The wind ironed her red cardigan flat against her slight body.The cardigan was buttoned up to her chin with tight little plastic rosebuds. Shirl fancied the river was rising. Bobbing sticks and leaves went swirling past. She pushed a stick into the mud. Chris pushed another little twig alongside the worried woman's marker. "Good boy. We'll test this old river."

Mick's horse stood cropping the grass and the hobbles' clink was blown into the wind as the animal moved a step or two at a time. The rushing wind made its coat shiver — cold, muddy brown.

Shirl was a placid woman. Calm and wise she went again to check the marker. The boy's had gone or was covered. Her own was now showing just the tip, and even as she looked it disappeared. She climbed the bank and said quietly to Joe, "We'll go to the Old Granny's. The river's up a bit."

Joe shouted to the kids. "Righto youse kids — we're going to the Old Granny's."

"What's wrong?" the younger kids wanted to know. And Shirl did not say anything.

As if to confirm the general feeling that something was wrong there was a hideous crackling of electricity like a rag being ripped and a roar of thunder that made everyone stand quite still.

"Jesus," said Joe.

Shirl and the kids set off, whipped by the wind across the flat. The Old Granny would know what to do.

By the time the party could see the shack great drops of icy rain were beginning to splash onto their skin. The old woman and Paula were around the back between the house and the river. Shirl and the children found them there.

The boy saw the Old Granny with her face set like a rock against the wind. She was encouraging the activities of Paula. The wind pulled at the great woman's clothes but her bulk seemed immoveable.

Without looking at the new arrivals the old woman said, "Youse come. Well reckon youse should go straight back to tent and wait for Jack. Flood's comin' but not yet. Reckon you go back and Jack will pack up, leave river. We goin' Pine Hill I reckon. That's right Paula, give it a good shake."

Paula was shaking the wire of the chicken coop. She was laughing. "Come on youse chooks — run away and save yaselfs. Get outa there."

The hens jerked sporadically about the scratched earth making urgent noises. Their small black eyes glistened and their white feathers were brilliant in the strange electric light pushed down by the heavy clouds. One hen suddenly found the opening and flapped out into its freedom. There was an instant following and the rest jammed and bustled in the doorway. As they rushed out there was an explosive separation of the birds. They fanned out in all directions and the coop was empty.

"Where they goin' Old Granny?" asked the boy.

The trees along the river were making a huge rushing noise. The grey wooden walls of the old shack were washed clean by the wind and the galvanised nails were polished cold.

"They probably gonna die!" shrieked Paula, "If they don't learn to fly real quick." And she laughed her enormous laugh.

The boy saw the retreating white feathers lifted up from behind and blown against the grain. Soon the hens disappeared, small and white and separate.

The Old Granny gave them a cup of hot tea and then bustled them outside into the wind. The air was exploding.

"Gee, there's gonna be a flood, everyone in town says." It was Sissy smiling and leaning on Mick. Brother and sister stumbled up to the veranda, cigarettes drooping from their mouths. Sissy looked windblown and drunk. "I thought you'd be over here. Good old Shirl, eh?"

Shirl looked at the floorboards.

"You look after them kids." The Old Granny spat the words at her daughter. "Paula and me goin' to Pine Hill. Reckon you and that Jack go to showgrounds."

"Wherever he is. Not at the tent." Sissy was smiling and her words were slurred.

"Sis and me just went there," said Mick and he drank the last from a sherry bottle he'd taken from his pocket.

"We was just going back," said Shirl quietly. "The Old Granny says the floods won't come yet."

"I can see that, I can see that." Sissy's mood was swinging as the grog did its tricks. "Hey — what 'bout a drink for ya little sister?"

"Sorry Sis, all gone." And Mick threw the bottle into the oleander bushes at the end of the veranda.

"You old meanie. Anyway there's gonna be a flood you know. I gotta get these kids back to their father and pack up the tent. There's gonna be a flood."

"Well git goin' then," said the Old Granny.

In time Sissy and Mick and the kids with Shirl made their bedraggled way back to the camp. It seemed the wind separated each one of them from the other. As the group came up to the tent they could see Jack doing something.

"What ya doin' my old man? Tightenin' the ropes? Well ya can just bloody untighten them 'cos we're not staying here to get drowned."

Chris felt frightened and eyed his father.

Sissy continued belligerent as the grog wore off. "There's gonna be a flood and I for one am pissin' off. And the kids are too."

Jack continued with his task of securing the tent pegs. He did not speak.

Sissy continued to build up like the storm all about, waving her arms wildly.

"What about you Shirl — you not staying here are ya?"

Shirl's eyes were downcast. The ribbing on her thin red cardigan ran between her flat breasts and the wind flattened her hair. She was silent. It was Mick who spoke.

"What ya reckon Jack? Reckon that river'll come up over the bank tonight?"

Jack spoke for the first time. "There's not gonna be a bloody flood — a bit of a downpour and everyone's runnin' round like a chook with its head cut off."

Mick had a bit of time for his brother-in-law but he said, "Gee mate — I don't know."

"Please yourself," and Jack started to hammer the pegs in again.

The grass cut the wind and the tight ropes shuddered in the air.

Chris felt fearful. Every hit his father gave to the pegs increased the tension in the air. His father was a solid wall of defiance.

"I reckon we'll pack up the wagon Jack," said Mick all of a sudden.

Jack kept securing the tent against the universe.

"Well piss off then!" Sissy threw the words at her brother like a stone. "Leave us here to drown — go to buggery."

"You could come too ..." Mick looked sideways at his brother-in-law.

"We'll be right, we'll be right."

So Mick and Shirl began piling stuff into the wagon. It did not take long. Mick harnessed up the horse and it looked impatient to be gone with the wind tearing at its mane and rattling the harness. Their two boys were lifted up inside the wagon. Mick and Shirl climbed up. They sat there foolishly hunched as the wind cut across them, Shirl's red cardigan was cold and thin.

Sissy would not look at them. Instead she walked off and sat on a flour drum with her back to the others.

Mick clicked his tongue a couple of times and the wagon jerked and then rolled away over the wet grass. The Leetons were alone with the river and the wind.

The night closed in and the river continued to swirl by, dark and dangerous. It became a beast that waited in the shadows, growling and threatening.

The man slapped some devon on four metal plates and cut some thick bread. After the kids had eaten he said. "Get into bed." They crawled under the blankets in their clothes and shut their eyes in a pretence of sleep. The rain beat solidly on the canvas. Sissy came into the tent then. The man lit the kerosene lantern and the tent shadow moved as the boy's parents sat there under that great wet sky, rolling cigarettes in their own private agonies.

In his half sleep Chris heard vague shufflings and mumblings as the man cursed and fumbled. He was pumping kerosene into the lantern. Jack adjusted the wick and the tent danced in a dull yellow light. The boy fell alseep.

When he awoke the world was chaotic. Gone was the soft light of the lantern. Now a great white light moved not within the tent but outside in the black and it picked up flying leaves and driving rain. Mixed with everything was the thudding of an engine.

"Hold me neck, that's it." His mum's voice.

"Here, give me that one." A strange voice — a man.

"How many are there?" Another man's voice — lower.

"Pass her up."

"Up you go."

"Here's another one."

Light in the boy's eyes. Cold cold rain on his face. Knees scraping on cold hard metal. Laughter.

"Here you go mate, get this round you."

Rough blanket down to bare feet which touched slatted boards.

Sissy's voice. "Yous sure ya got four up there? Don't youse move this bloody thing till I've counted them."

"We're not leaving anyone." Serious voice — like telling off.

"All here, righto, best take her over towards the bridge." Strange voice of authority. Beating cold rain. Swirling world in black moving night.

"Youse kids alright?" Sissy's voice — softer now — less edgy.

The floating vibrating machine with its strong white light pushed its way through the flood. There seemed to be a great many people. They sat on the slatted seats of the machine, all safe. The machine floated towards the approaches to the bridge. Its wheels fluttered as they found the solid wooden planks. It rumbled across and Chris saw the great white triangles slowly moving overhead. Above the whining engine and the driving rain a soldier shouted,

"Jesus, it's a floating farm out there — chooks and everything."

It was the smell more than anything that seemed to wrap around the boy and claim him and yet exclude him by its strangeness. It was a smell of damp and cloying heat, of cabbage and wet concrete. The echoing tin hall was filled with people. Practically the whole of the northern side of the town's population had arrived at the showground. But the Old Granny, the great Paula, Billy and Prince and all the other people were nowhere to be seen. The rest had been rescued by the Army — as the Leetons had. They'd arrrived by tractors, horse drawn carts, on foot, car and even bicycles. They clustered in groups under the thundering corrugated iron roof of the pavilion. In other summers the same people had wandered through this hall, commenting on the vegetables and animals and flowers which they raised in the surrounding countryside and which gave meaning to their existence within the landscape.

All the people were together under the glaring bare bulbs which hung from the cobwebbed angle-iron high above. Some sat on forms waiting to be ordered around. Children slept on the bare concrete covered with coats or whatever was at hand. At the end of the pavilion stood a long trestle table with tall piles of thick white china plates and cups.

The flood had tumbled down the river in the night and no one had had time to sandbag their houses or lift sideboards onto drums. Many of the people muttered about the Godforsaken land and how they were going to pack up and go. How they didn't belong. How they were losing their fight with the land. Of course afterwards they would go and push out the mud and scrub down their walls and grow old and bitter in the memory of their losses.

No one understood the floods except the other people of the river. *They lived not by a river but in the whole world. The landscape was not separated into hills, valleys, rivers, flats. The river was the sky. It lived for a time in the sky. But there was no time. It hid and played under the dry flats and flowed across the face of the burning sun. It filled the space between the stars and as the whole great play of light and dark, of shifting water and wind-swept earth rolled around with its birds and lizards, kangaroos and snakes, everyone moved effortlessly like shadows in the bush, just as the sun moved away for the wind. Floods do not arrive either catastrophically or quietly — they are always here. The river is a tide.*

Sissy looked at the wet miserable huddle of people: Jack was standing over with his sister. She looked at her kids. She felt lost.

Sissy was a small girl. The river was in flood. The sky was black as she walked up the hill with Paula. She held Paula's sweaty hand. She was wrapped around with love.

Pine Hill: the Old Granny and Paula were there now. Not here with strangers in a raining night all wrapped up in Army blankets. So she cursed the man. She knew she was alone.

But she remembered, half remembered when everything just was.

She walked up the hill to Aunty's. The floods swirled in the droughts and the earth was parched in flood. The sun shone at night and the moon whitened the world by day. There was no yesterday or tomorrow. Now was when Paula let the chooks out. Now was when they sat up at Pine Hill eating damper with the big quiet faces all around.

She hated these people because she did not belong. Did she belong with the big quiet faces?

She wanted to run. She wanted to smash the tall towers of white plates and run away into where the shattered fragments of white crockery fell quietly, and as they fell they changed into a broad hot white plain where two still kangaroos with little burnt front paws stared across the distance — across all time — and stared at her in the eternal silence. And all was alright again.

Sissy knew then that she would leave Jack. She could see him now talking with his tight-haired sister who nervously clutched a large green handbag. Sissy knew that Jack and his sister were silently cursing the river. But Sissy did not curse the river. She cursed the man. Sissy was not one with the river, but she understood her mother, and as Sissy would have said, her mother understood the river. Unlike the man, Sissy had an instinct for survival. But her bitterness grew when she finally realised she could never go back to when she hadn't seen the difference between her mother and herself.

"Only the whites drown — unless they take us too," her thoughts were abjectly bitter.

And her bitterness and hatred and self-doubt all came together in a sickening surge of half-knowledge that made it impossible for her to hold on to any concept of "us".

Earlier that day, when Sissy had told Jack that the river would flood, her words had been utterly unable to cross that vast gulf between her world and her husband's.

The waters receded. The people went back to their private battles. The Leeton family was dropped off at Waterbag Road by Mr Dawson. (It was Mr Dawson who had employed Jack at the garage.) The dwelling was one main room with a corrugated iron lean-to attached. At one end of the lean-to was a flimsy tin cooking area. The main room, where cows had been milked, still had a few stray bolts sticking up from the concrete floor where a separator once stood. There was one window overlooking a red dirt lane running by a wheat field. Outside was a furphy which Dawson would tow away every now and then to refill at the cattle trough.

The family settled in and the sun shone. The wheat across in the paddock turned from electric green to rusty gold. The lane glowed rose pink as the surface dried out and broke up.

The hot Christmas arrived and settled with its magic and flies over the landscape. The small gums scattered down the lane stood milky green. Sissy took the kids and they broke off a branch. Back in the shed they decorated it with coloured paper. Sissy cut *"Merry Christmas"* from pretty paper and strung it across the top of the window.

The wind moved over the ripening wheat and lifted the light paper message.

The kids had fizzy drinks and Sissy and Jack floated bottles of beer in the cool water of the furphy. Later in the afternoon there was a summer storm and heavy rain drops punched into the red earth and washed the gum leaves. The family moved inside and the smell of dust and rain came through the window and all the wheat across the lane moved as the storm rolled in from the west.

It was the last Christmas before Sydney. Chris asked why his name sounded like Christmas. Sissy and Jack laughed because they didn't know.

Author Notes

LARISSA BEHRENDT, born in 1969, is Professor of Law and Indigenous Studies and director of the Jumbunna Indigenous House of Learning at the University of Technology Sydney. She graduated from University of New South Wales Law School in 1992 and has since completed her Master of Law and Doctorate at Harvard Law School. A practicing lawyer and lecturer, she has worked with the United Nations. She is on the Aboriginal and Torres Strait Islander Council national Treaty Think Tank and has served on the ACT Bill of Rights Inquiry. In 2003 her book based on her doctoral thesis *Achieving Social Justice: Indigenous Rights and Australia's Future* was released by Federation Press, publisher of her first book *Aboriginal Dispute Resolution*, 1995.

Her novel *Home,*which won the 2002 Unaipon Award and will soon be published, evolved from the need to maintain her connection with home and family while living overseas. The legend of the Mea-Mei, which appears in this anthology, is from her family's Eualeyai/Kamillaroi heritage and was told to her as a child by her father.

LISA BELLEAR, born 1950 in Melbourne, is a descendent of the Goernpil/Noonuccal of Stradbroke Island, Queensland. A poet, writer, visual artist, academic and social commentator, her works present a unique style of Australian art. She has been writing and performing poetry for more than thirty years.

Her first collection of poetry *Dreaming in Urban Areas* was published in 1996. She was a volunteer broadcaster with 3CR Community Radio's 'Not Another Koori Show' for eighteen years, and in

1999 completed an MA in Creative Writing at University of Queensland. She is currently a Lecturer at Victoria University of Technology (School of Education) and a PhD student at La Trobe University. Lisa writes to challenge the status quo on human rights, sovereignty, Land Rights and women's rights; and to give a voice to Murries and non-Murries who feel their concerns are not heard.

JOHN MUK MUK BURKE was born in Narrandera, New South Wales in 1946, of a Wiradjuri mother and an Irish father. He left school at fifteen and spent some years working for the post office before going to New Zealand on a working holiday. After a number of jobs ranging from scrub clearing to factory work he was accepted into Auckland Teachers' College in 1967. He has taught in primary schools in New Zealand, Darwin and outback Northern Territory, and has been a specialist art teacher and music advisor for the Northern Territory Department of Education. He was a lecturer in History and English Literature at the Centre for Aboriginal and Islander Studies at the Northern Territory University from 1992 to 2001.

In 1989 he took a year off to travel in Europe, and it was in France that the first draft of *Bridge of Triangles* was written. It was chosen as the winner of the 1993 Unaipon Award. His poetry volume *Night Song and Other Poems* won the national Kate Challis RAKA Award in 2000. He is currently writing his next novel and working as a teacher at the Goulburn Correctional Centre with Aboriginal inmates, gaining inspiration from their personal stories.

VIVIENNE CLEVEN was born in 1968 in Surat, Queensland, and grew up in western Queensland, homeland of her Aboriginal heritage. She left school at the age of thirteen to work with her father as a jillaroo:

building fences, mustering cattle, and working at various jobs on stations throughout Queensland and New South Wales.

In 2000, with the manuscript *Bitin' Back*, Vivienne Cleven entered and won the David Unaipon Award. Published the following year, *Bitin' Back* was shortlisted in the 2002 *Courier-Mail* Book of the Year Award and in the 2002 South Australian Premier's Award for Fiction. In the latter shortlist, *Bitin' Back* was listed with Peter Carey's *True History of the Kelly Gang*, which won. She wrote the playscript for *Bitin' Back*, which will be performed by Brisbane's Kooemba Jdarra Indigenous Theatre Company. *Her Sister's Eye* was published in 2002 and was chosen in the 2003 People's Choice shortlist of One Book One Brisbane.

JACK DAVIS (1917-1999) began writing when he was fourteen years old. The fourth child in a family of eleven, he spent his childhood in the West Australian mill town of Yarloop. He worked for several years as a stockman in the north before returning to Perth and settling into fulltime writing and a long life of service to the Aboriginal cause.

His book publications began in 1970 with *The First Born*, a volume of poetry. *Jagardoo: Poems from Aboriginal Australia* (1978) and *John Pat and Other Poems* (1988) followed. His plays include *No Sugar, Burungin, Honeyspot, Kullark* and *The Dreamers* and *Our Town*. In 1991 his memoir *A Boy's Life* was published. He has received numerous distinctions including the British Empire Medal, the Order of Australia, honorary doctorates from the universities of Murdoch and Western Australia. An inaugural Unaipon Award judge, he served as judge on the panel from 1988 to 1996.

GRAEME DIXON was born in Perth in 1955. His mother is a Noongar from Katanning and his father an English migrant orphan who grew up at Fairbridge Farm. Beginning at three years of age, he spent several years in Sister Kate's Children's Home. Between ten and fourteen years he lived in a Salvation Army Boys Home, before being expelled from high school. He was in and out of reformatories and at sixteen ended up in Fremantle Prison where he spent most of the next nine years. He began writing while in prison, where restrictions made it necessary for him to hide his poetry from the authorities.

At twenty-seven, Graeme began tertiary study and later completed a course at Curtin University on politics, communications and Aboriginal Studies. In 1999 his first collection of poetry *Holocaust Island* won the Unaipon Award. He has written on his life in the 2002 University of Western Australia publication *Echoes of the Past: Sister Kate's Home Revisited*; and is currently writing his memoir.

JOHN GRAHAM, born in 1969, grew up in Brisbane and lives on the Gold Coast. His ancestors are Kombumeri and Waka Waka, Irish, Scottish and English. *Land Window* was chosen as a Highly Commended entry by the Unaipon judges and was published in 1998.

John is also an artist and musician. His art includes commissioned sketches and illustrations in his book *Land Window*. As a musician, he has studied music and performed with bands; and was second place winner of the Gold Coast Great Guitars competition. He has worked as a labourer, surveyor and map maker; and has lived in South Australia, Western Australia and Far North Queensland.

ELIZABETH HODGSON lives in Wollongong, on the New South Wales south coast. Born in 1956, she spent her childhood in Sydney in a State Home for fair-skinned Aboriginal children. She writes from the perspective of a fair-skinned woman with a dark-skinned father about the racism which has permeated every aspect of her life.

Her collection of poems *Skin Painting* was Highly Commended in the 2002 Unaipon Award.

MELISSA LUCASHENKO, a Murri woman of European and Ygambeh/Bundjalung descent, has affiliations with the Arrente and Waanyi people. She was born in Brisbane in 1967 and grew up on its southern outskirts. After working as a bar attendant, housepainter and martial arts instructor, she received an Honours Degree in Public Policy from Griffith University and has since lived in Canberra, Darwin, the Kingdom of Tonga and on the north coast of New South Wales.

Her first book *Steam Pigs* won the 1998 Dobbie Award for Women's Fiction and was shortlisted for the 1999 New South Wales Premier's fiction award and the Commonwealth Writer's Prize, First Published Book. Her next book *Killing Darcy* won the Children's Book Council Award and the Royal Blind Society's Talking Book Award for young readers. *Hard Yards* was published in 1999 and shortlisted in the 2002 *Courier-Mail* Best Book Award. In 2002 her fourth book *Too Flash* was launched by Jukurrpa Books.

DORIS PILKINGTON's traditional name is Nugi Garimara. She was born in 1937 on Balfour Downs Station in the East Pilbara, homeland of her Mardu ancestors. As a toddler she was removed by authorities from her home at the station, along with her mother Molly Craig and baby sister Anna, and committed to Moore River Native Settlement. This was the same institution Molly had escaped from ten years previously, the account of which is told in *Follow the Rabbit Proof Fence*.

At eighteen, Doris left the mission system as the first of its members to qualify for the Royal Perth Hospital's nursing aide training program. Following marriage and a family, she studied journalism and worked in film/video production. *Caprice: A Stockman's Daughter*, originally published in 1991, is her first book and won the 1990 Unaipon Award. Her second book *Follow the Rabbit-Proof Fence* was first published in 1996 and has been reprinted several times since the international release of the film 'Rabbit-Proof Fence' in 2002. Doris has travelled extensively throughout the world with the film's director Phillip Noyce. *Under the Wintamarra Tree,* her third book and the story of her journey back to her family and traditional homeland, was launched in 2002. She is Co-Patron of State and Federal Sorry Day Committees' Journey of Healing.

SAMUEL WAGAN WATSON, born in 1972, is a descendant of the Mununjali and the Birri Guba. His first collection of poetry, *Of Muse, Meandering and Midnight*, won the 1999 Unaipon Award. After publication it received a Highly Commended in both the Anne Elder Award and the 2000 Award for Outstanding Contributions to Australian Culture. *Itinerant Blues* was published in 2001.

He is also co-author of the Brisbane City Council website *blackfellas, whitefellas, wetlands*; and his chapbook, *hotel bone*, was published in 2001. Samuel has been a guest of literary festivals and poetry readings in Europe and throughout Australia and in New Zealand.

HERB WHARTON, born in 1936 in Cunnamulla, Queensland, began his working life as a drover while in his teens. His maternal grandmother was of the Kooma people; his grandfathers were Irish and English. In 1992 with the publication of his first book *Unbranded,* he committed to novel form his experiences of people and events from his long years on the stock routes of inland Australia. His next book *Cattle Camp*, a collection of droving stories as told by Murri stockmen and women, was published in 1994. *Where Ya' Been, Mate?*, a collection of his stories, followed in 1996.

He has travelled throughout Australia, and to Europe and Japan. In 1998 he was selected for a residency at the Australia Council studio in Paris where he completed the manuscript of *Yumba Days*, his first book for young readers, published in 1999.

ALEXIS WRIGHT was born in 1950 in Cloncurry, Queensland, and currently lives in Alice Springs. Her tribal affiliations are with the Waanyi people of the highlands of the southern Gulf of Carpentaria. She has held a range of management, education research and writing positions revolving around Indigenous land and culture issues, and cross-cultural concerns in relation to conflict resolution and regional planning.

Her other books are *Grog War*, which documents the achievements of the Waramangu people in their campaign to restrict alcohol in Tennant Creek; *Take Power*, an anthology of essays and stories celebrating twenty years of Land Rights in Central Australia; published in France: *La pacte du serpent arc-en-ciel*, her collection of short stories, and *Croire en l'incroyable*, a nonfiction book series *Le souffle de l'esprit*. She has completed a second novel, a sweeping epic appropriately entitled *Carpentaria*.

"In my traditional homeland in Gulf of Carpentaria we speak of hearing only one heart beat. To hear this heart beat of the land our heart beat must be in unison with it. My novels *Plains of Promise* and *Carpentaria* have been a search through the characters and plots I have chosen and created in fiction to dig through contemporary circumstances, through history, to rejoice in the spaces where our culture and identity breathes. The aim of this fiction is to bring to the ears of the world the heavy pulse of our Waanyi nation and to amplify its sounds." — A.W.

DAVID UNAIPON was the first Indigenous writer to be published in Australia. He was born in 1872 at Point McLeay Mission on the lower Murray River in South Australia, home to the Ngarrindjeri. Educated in the classics, religion and science, he was an inventor, scientist and writer. He wrote speeches and published pamphlets, and travelled throughout South Australia collecting and writing traditional stories. A collection of his stories written between 1924 and 1925 and entitled 'Legendary Tales of the Australian Aborigines' is held in the State Library of New South Wales. He died in 1967, three years after the next Indigenous writer, Kath Walker (later Oodgeroo), was published.

Only recently brought to light is the literary appropriation of the edited stories from the State Library collection, which were published in 1930 in England as *Myths & Legends of the Australian Aboriginals* and attributed to W. Ramsay Smith, the alias of a non-Indigenous medical officer and professional associate of David Unaipon.

Black Australian Writing Series

Since 1988 with the establishment of the David Unaipon competition, which discovers new Aboriginal and Torres Strait Islander writers, UQP has built up an international reputation as the largest publisher of books by Indigenous authors in Australia. UQP's Black Australian Writing series evolved out the Unaipon Award and today includes Indigenous-authored books which range from novels and poetry to lifestories and essays. Through the combined expertise of our authors, cultural advisors and specialist staff, UQP continues in its commitment to Indigenous writing as a valued contribution to the literature of a nation.